Anjoy—God's Gifts

Jill Divine

PublishAmerica
Baltimore

First printing

ISBN: 1-4137-6465-7
PUBLISHED BY PUBLISHAMERICA, LLLP
www.publishamerica.com
Baltimore

Printed in the United States of America

Dedication and Acknowledgments

I would like to thank the angels for their continued support. Even when I gave up and lost my trust in them they made sure I always knew they were there.

Carol Green, for helping me expand my psychic abilities to a level that Tracey-Jane Rees was then able to show me how to raise them even higher and finally listen and speak to the angels.

Lastly and most importantly of all, to my wonderful son, David, who has, I hesitate to say, patiently taught me to use the computer and put up with my many blunders!

Finally, before my many friends say, "And what about me?" Yes, I would like to thank you all for keeping my spirit and energy positive.

Love and light

Jill Divine

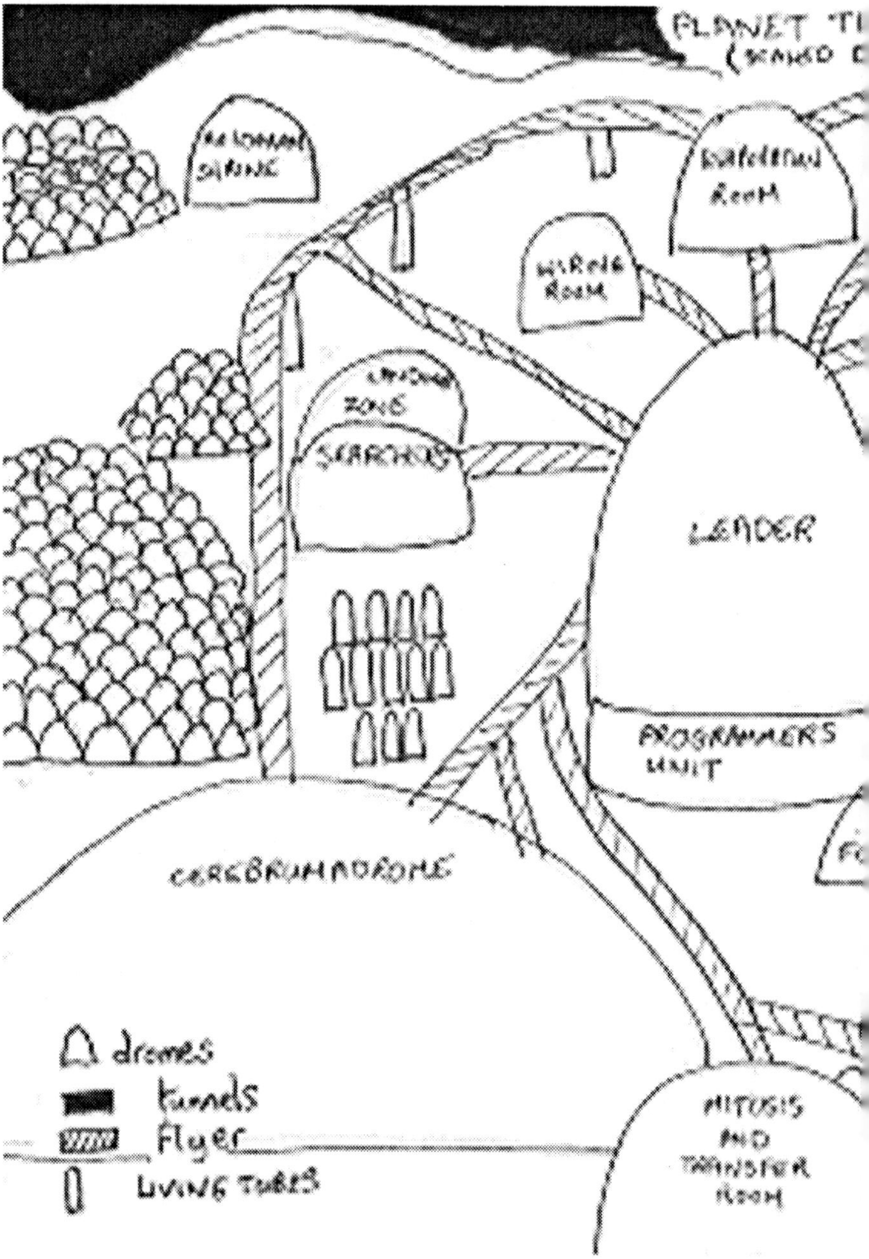
PLANET
SEARCHERS
LEADER
PROGRAMMERS UNIT
CEREBRUMADROME
MITOSIS AND TRANSFER ROOM
dromes
tunnels
Flyer
LIVING TUBES

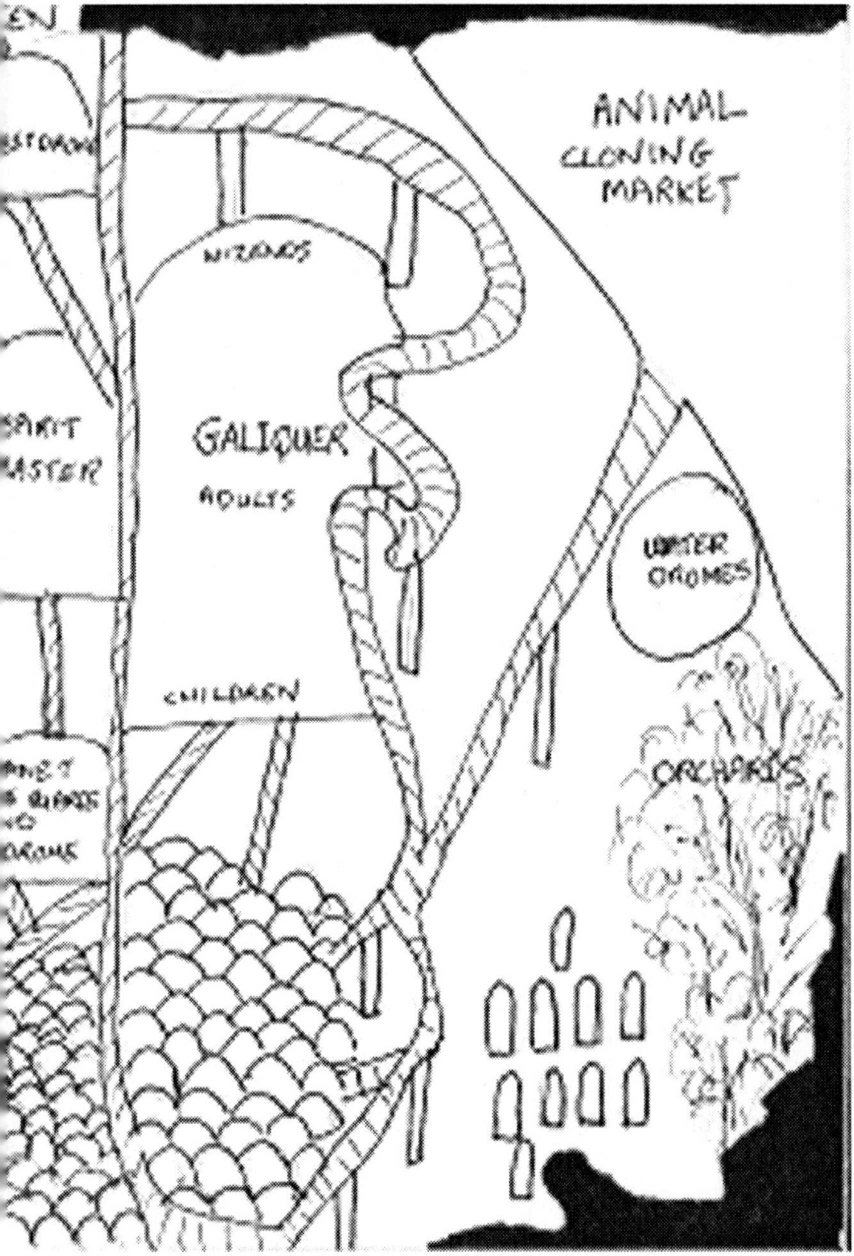
ANIMAL
CLONING
MARKET
GALIQUER
ADULTS
CHILDREN
ORCHARDS

Chapter 1

Planet Tirleen, Year 3030
(Population: Always 20,000)

The Spirit Master opened his bleary eyes. God, he was tired. He wasn't a fanciful man given to dreaming at night. In fact, it should have been impossible for him to dream, or so he thought. Until now. Every night it was the same dream, or perhaps a nightmare. Not ever having had any of these before, he wasn't sure.

An angel had stood at the bottom of his bed every single night this week, telling him to listen. A great miracle was going to happen, and he was to assist in a great way. God was fed up with people not believing in him. Too few people were attending church and too many down at the pub getting drunk.

Perhaps he was eating too many mince pies at the Giving plays? As the Spirit Master he was obliged to attend every one of them, and as it involved the children getting drunk, which they loved, there were many of them! It was based on the nativity play, something that was performed at this time every year in the past, many, many years ago. Only Given was then called Christmas. In the past, people had this weird notion that there was a man called God and that he'd not only actually created the whole world, but he had sent his son down to earth. They thought this son was born on Christmas day, and he would save the world!

He chuckled to himself at the word "whole," thinking how stupid the people must have been to imagine there was one man, who no one had ever seen, who could create the whole universe! They also had this weird idea that when you died you met your loved ones and could even be reborn, so could live many lives. Of course, since then there had been many wars and now there was only their planet, Tirleen, left. So if this God had existed, why had he let this happen and where were all these people who were reborn?

Their leader, Zut, decided when new life was to be created and chose whether it was the male or female whose cells were used to create one. Apparently in God's days, only the females gave birth and they had to carry it inside them for nine whole months! How they gave birth to it was the most gruesome and torturous method he'd ever heard of. Any person, God or otherwise, who allowed a person to suffer such torture was a very cruel man indeed.

No, thank goodness he was the Spirit Master. It was his job to teach the children that this was all rubbish and there never was such a person as God. He was just a fairy tale made up by people who lived in big houses and took lots of money off people by making them go to places called church and then actually preaching to them and telling them they mustn't drink and also forgo all the good things in life.

At least people had come to their senses many, many years ago and realized that if there was a God he would have stopped all these wars and people dying. It was all down to their great leader Zut's ancestors that people had finally realized the truth. Zut's ancestors were a most intelligent race and each generation had become more and more evolved and had shown everyone how to live differently and better.

So, now he had to attend the Giving plays and watch the children mocking the old nativity play by giving each other loads of presents and getting drunk on the celestdrome to celebrate the birth of this poor baby called Jesus. The fairy tale said he had been born to save the world and then had been nailed to a cross and killed instead! Well, he would just have to get drunk, but avoid those awful sickly mince pies that everyone made as a joke.

Yes, that was the answer, no more of those disgusting mince pies. They certainly sat heavily on the stomach at night, so that was probably why he was starting to dream. Perhaps they contained something that switched the brainwaves on at night. Their brain was normally programmed to switch off at night so it was impossible to dream. He must get these mince pies analysed and see what was in them. Perhaps it was a ploy by the Faith Believers to get into their minds and brainwash everyone to start them believing in God again?

He shuddered as he thought of the Faith Believers. There was only a few of them and they were nearly all the wizend people. Thankfully, as they were all in their late hundreds or early two hundreds, their time was nearly up, as everyone died on their two hundred and fiftieth birthday.

The Faith Believers held secret Faith meetings in hidden tunnels and carried on with this belief that God still lived and would one day save them all again. They'd managed to find a few of their hiding places and had captured them and put them in sealed tubes, which kept them alive and then put on public display, where they would stay until they were two hundred and fifty and died. He hoped that would deter the rest of the Faith Believers.

Now he was satisfied that he'd worked out what was causing these dreams, he got up and walked into the cleansing room, which would wash and dry him before breakfast. He made a mental note to look up one of the words that the angel had said, "pub." He'd never heard this word before and wondered where it was and why it made this imaginary God so cross.

Chapter 2
Beating the Odds

"Don't forget to visit wizend Edril after school," Viola shouted as Ashtez and Hurlen were leaving to catch the flier to the cerebrumadrome.

"Do we have to?" said Ashtez, groaning. "She's at least two hundred and always moaning about how she used to attend church at Christmas and it should be about giving, not receiving," Ashtez moaned.

"She is not that old. One hundred and fifteen is quite young and just be respectful to her. Remember, she's your wizend," their mother shouted after them.

The flier was crowded, but Hurlen quickly found some empty seats for the two of them. Ashtez made herself comfortable and tuned her contact gaming lenses in and instructed her brain to play. "Yuck, having to visit smelly old wizend. If she *gave* us a present, I'm sure she'd *receive* a thank you," she said, screaming with laughter to her brother. She thought this remark was so funny that whilst she was having hysterics laughing at herself, she dislodged her right gaming lens. This sent the game all blurry in front of her eyes and made her feel quite dizzy. She licked her finger and stuck the gaming lens back in place and continued to battle with the robot wires.

"How do you get past that orange and black ziggy wire that's attached to their eye to get into their brain?" said Hurlen, who looked as if he was staring into space, but along with all the other children on the flier was concentrating on the game they were playing on their lens.

"Visualize another one attached to it, and it will confuse the robot. Then you can jump into their brain," she replied whilst trying not to lose her concentration.

She was almost in the middle of the robot's brain, which meant she only had a short way to go to the spinal wires, and once there she could laser them and collapse the robot all together, making her the winner, yet again.

She was glad that she'd opted out of this year's Giving play, as all that galiquon gave you a violent headache the next day. It was bad enough having to spend sixty wixons at cerebrumadrome every single day until they were twenty-five, but when you had a thumping headache it just got worse when they attached the lead to the fourth lobe of your cerebrum and it was filled with that day's knowledge and learning.

She was looking forward to today because the last wixon was gaming time. This was why she and all the other children were staring into space as they travelled today. They had all brought their gaming lens with them ready to go head to head with the hidden robot lens. This was a treat for them as it was nearly Given and they would have one day off cerebrumadrome. *Absolute bliss*, she thought. She could spend all day gaming and hoped her hinting for the twelve latest gaming lenses had been heard by her parents. She wanted to go through all of them before Given day ended and it was back to cerebrumadrome.

She was confident she was going to find the hidden robot lens today and get into its brain and sever its spinal cord. No one had found its new hiding place for years, but she had been using her wire knowledge and felt sure it was hidden in the middle of the pons varolein that was located at the base of the cerebrumadrome's energy wire.

Their leader had obviously thought he was very clever hiding the hidden robot lens in the middle of the place that taught them every day. Everyone normally hunted around the walls, the floor and the ceiling, thinking it was bound to be hiding somewhere in one of those places. Well, she'd finally caught him out. She would show him that she was as intelligent as he was and perhaps he'd remember her name when it was time for her to join the Planet Force when she was twenty-five years old.

She was hoping to be a Searcher, but only the most intelligent of the Tirleen's race became Searchers. It involved going off for long periods in spaceships and hunting for other races and planets. Zut was not convinced that every planet and race had died out, so the Searcher's job was to find any other life form and bring it back to Tirleen so that he could clone it. She desperately wanted to be the first person to find the life form, but it was another thirteen years before she was twenty-five and joined the Planet Force. She hoped no one found any before she reached that age, plus she had to prove how clever she was before then to Zut so that he would remember her. She must find the hidden gaming lens today!

It was a pity that God did not exist, she thought. Then perhaps one of these prayers the stories talked about could be used and would find the hidden gaming lens for her. But, of course, as he was only a character in a fairy tale, it would be no use praying to him anyhow because it wouldn't be heard. She hoped that their wizend didn't start whining on about remembering what Given really meant and trying to get her to go to one of her secret Faith meetings. Ashtez was terrified that the Spirit Master would find out that their wizend was a Faith Believer and went to Faith meetings. It could affect her whole future. Zut would never give her the position of Searcher if he knew one of their family was a Faith Believer.

She was also a little worried that Viola, their mother, had been persuaded to attend some of these meetings. She seemed to keep sneaking off and was very secretative about where she was going. Dad didn't know where she went, and thankfully he hated Faith Believers, so he certainly hadn't been persuaded by the wizend to go.

He would be very cross with Viola if he found out that she had been to any.

The flier stopped in the middle of the cerebrumadrome and everyone was teleported and placed onto their seats. Then the leads came down and plugged straight into the fourth lobe of all the children's cerebrum. This was the centre of all their learning, and information was sent straight down the leads and into the wires of their brain. What information they received depended upon how old they were and what information they had to receive that day.

Everyone attended cerebrumadrome from the first day of their birth to the age of twenty-five, and depending on their age, only received the strength of information that their brain was able to tolerate. The information was fed into all the wires and neurons and made it impossible for your mind to wander, or if it did, you were given a jolt to bring you back into the learning state.

Ashtez was so excited about finding the hidden robot lens that she allowed her mind to wander several times as she visualized how she was going to get into the pons varolein. She received several jolts, which made her brain ache like mad. She really must not let her brain wander. She needed to concentrate as hard as possible to win today and she didn't need a thumping headache that would only hinder her.

Ashtez breathed a sigh of relief as exactly fifty-nine wixons later the lights went off all the leads leading into their brain. This was the signal for everyone to put their gaming lens in and start the hunt for the hidden robot lens. The air was full of excitement as everyone hurried to put their lens in. This was a real treat and only happened once a year at Given, as it was Zut's gift to all the children.

The instance all the leads lit up again, everyone stared into space as they concentrated hard on finding the hidden robot lens. Ashtez went straight for the cerebrumadrome's brain and quickly reached the grey wires. She couldn't waste any time and had to find a way to the pons varolein as quickly as possible. She panicked as the grey wire shocked her and sent her lens all blurry. *Phew! That was too close for comfort,* she thought as she shook her head and regained her vision. She was only in the second lobe of the robot's brain. She couldn't get killed so early in the game!

As she traveled down the grey wire a thought popped into her head. Why was the grey wire attacking? The grey wire was normally peaceful and protected you from the vicious white wires. The robot brain must be on to her. He'd realised she knew where the lens was and was playing dirty to stop her. Wow! She was excited now, if it was a battle he wanted, then that was what he'd get. The adrenaline pumped through her body as she cruised through all the wires. She was going to get that hidden lens however tough it was.

Suddenly she found herself battling with several gyri wires hidden in the folds of the robot's brain. They had tried to take her, thinking she wasn't concentrating, but she had been alert and waiting for them. As she severed the gyri wires a band of sylci wires surrounded her. She'd fallen into a fissure. *Don't panic,* she kept telling herself. She could do it.

"Help!" she yelled out aloud as she found herself spinning and going quite dizzy. She felt so sick it was difficult to concentrate. At the bottom of the fissure she'd fallen into was the jelly river surrounding the Island of Reilas, and she was being whirled round and round it and turned from side to side, almost tipping over. She had to take control quickly because if they tipped her over, which was obviously what they were trying to do, she would drown in the jelly river. It was really hard to keep upright as she was tipped and turned around. Thank goodness one of her favourite gaming lens was *Circuitry of the Blue Rapids.* She was an expert at that and had been spun round the rapids of wire so many times that it was now getting boring and she was going to pass the lens onto Hurlen.

Just pretend it's the blue rapids she kept telling herself over and over again. Suddenly to her relief, she spotted an open wire leading to the cerebelter entrance. She leaned over and grabbed one of the red wires, then swung herself into the opening. This was much better; all was quiet in here. She could compose herself and get her concentration back. The quietness was soothing and calming and Ashtez wondered why it was so quiet. The robot knew she was very near now. Why wasn't he attacking? She only had to slide down the pitruitadrome tunnel and then she could jump into the pons varolein and quickly sever the wire surrounding it and win the game.

The quietness became hypnotic and Ashtez found she was starting to blink and nearly dislodged the lens. She took a very deep breath and made herself concentrate again. Now she knew what he was doing. He was hypnotising her so that her brain stopped thinking and then he was going to jump in and sever her connection and beat her. Well, she certainly wasn't going to fall for that trick. She hadn't come this far to lose at the last wire.

A light appeared in front of her and she could see the top of the pitruitadrome tunnel. She grabbed a grey and purple wire and held on tightly as it slid down the tunnel. She let go at the bottom and as the pons varolein opened up, she dived in. Before the robot lens could attack, she severed the wires surrounding it. A feeling of elation flooded through her body. She'd done it! She'd won. She'd actually beaten the odds and not only found the hidden robot lens, but beaten it.

The sound of cheering and clapping rang in her ears and Ashtez realized it was for her, but as she was basking in the glory, she found herself being teleported and then staring into their leader's smiling face.

Chapter 3
Sirleen Finds His Miracle

"Dad, where's Mum? I want to know what to do with these disgusting mince pies the wizend sent for her!" shouted Ashtez as she was teleported into their drome.

"She's at the Hologram Shrine saying goodbye to your sister," Odraine replied sadly.

"God, that place is so creepy. I don't know why our leader ever set it up," she said, grimacing.

"Because he felt guilty that the acceleration process went wrong and so many babies died. He built it so that they could see what their children would look like if they'd lived."

Ashtez shuddered at the thought of a vision floating in front of you. She knew they were only holograms created by the computer using their family likeness and changing the person as they grew, but just the thought of it made her body quiver. Why their leader had ever decided to build such a place she would never know. Death was final. So what if those babies died? No one had known them, so what was all the fuss about? Her parents had only waited a few weeks after her sister's death and she had been created. *Thankfully,* she thought, from her father this time. At least she had more of his strong genes than her mother's. Which was probably why she was so clever. Still, her mother wouldn't be able to go to that creepy Hologram Shrine for much longer, as their leader had finally come to his senses and was destroying it tomorrow.

"Dad stop thinking of her and ask me how I got on today," she said impatiently."

"By 'her,' I presume you mean Anjoy?" he said crossly, wishing he'd gone with Viola to say goodbye to their daughter.

"Anjoy, 'her,' whatever you want to call her," she said casually. To her it had seemed odd naming something that was dead, so she never referred to her by name, only "her."

"She's your sister," Odraine replied, trying to keep calm. Hurlen and Ashtez always referred to Anjoy as "her." It was very upsetting. They just didn't seem to understand how sad it had been when Anjoy had died.

"If you say so, but it's a bit like naming something you've just eaten. Once you've swallowed it, it's gone. You don't say, 'Sorry, how are you feeling now Jamina,' or whatever you want to call it," she said arrogantly. She was feeling very put-out now. All her father could think of was Anjoy, who didn't exist, whereas she did, and she had the best news ever to share with him. Why didn't he shut up about that stupid person?

"Ashtez!" her father said, very shocked at what he'd just heard.

He looked like he was going to have a hissy fit, so Ashtez quickly used all her diplomatic skills to calm him down.

"Oh, Dad, I'm really sorry. That was very unfeeling of me. Of course Anjoy is our sister and it's only because I would dearly have loved to have a big sister." She paused here for a bit of dramatic affect. "I miss her too, you know." At this she made a few tears come into her eyes and hoped this would do the trick.

Her father calmed down instantly as he realized that Anjoy's death had obviously affected their other children too, only they were much better at hiding their feelings than he and Viola were.

As her father hugged her, Ashtez beamed with pride. She was a good actress, she thought. She would need a lot of diplomatic skills if she became a Searcher, because if she ever found life forms she needed to be very clever to find out if they were friendly or not. Yes, she was very pleased with herself. Her dad was pacified and she'd proved how good she could be. Well, if she could fool her dad, then she could definitely fool any aliens she found!

Ashtez unpacked all her lenses and stored them in the wall to keep them sterile and free from specks of dust which could distort any information stored on them. As he watched her, Odraine suddenly remembered how excited she was when she came home and obviously had some good news to tell him, but he'd been wallowing in grief at the thought of never seeing Anjoy again. Ashtez was right, whatever was wrong with him? Anjoy was dead and she'd died a long time ago. What was he doing still grieving over something that was dead?

It was the wizend's fault for going on about God punishing them for not believing in him. She might be Viola's wizend, but they would have to stop visiting her if she kept trying to push this God business on them. Thankfully his wizends weren't like that. They hated the Faith Believers and if they knew Viola's wizend was one, they would report it to Zut. She was becoming a liability and could put all the family in danger if Zut every found out about it.

He knew Ashtez desperately wanted to be a Searcher and even though it was thirteen years away, he felt sure she would make the grade. She had more of his genes in her. He beamed with pride at the thought of it. He was glad he'd been chosen to create the life of their next child. His friends were right, you did feel closer to them if you were the one chosen to use the main cell from.

"So how did you get on at cerebrumadrome then?" Odraine finally asked Ashtez.

She grinned with delight. At last she could share her good news with her father. She was a lot closer to him than her mother and desperately wanted to tell him first, so she'd been very pleased when she learned that her mother was at the Hologram Shrine visiting her creepy "sister" and Hurlen was at the celestdrome practicing the Giving Play.

"I found it, Dad, I found it!" she screamed with joy as she jumped all around the room.

"You found the hidden robot lens?" he said, utterly shocked. It was practically unheard of for anyone to find it and it had only been found three times in the last century. Zut was very clever and always hid it where he knew no brains would ever work out where it was.

"Wow!" he said. He didn't know what else to say. He was so proud of his daughter. *His daughter,* he thought. She was definitely "his daughter."

"I really can't believe you found it. Do you know how incredible that is? The odds of finding it are almost impossible."

Ashtez beamed. She was so happy she could barely speak. She'd found the hidden robot lens! She could still remember being instantly teleported to their leader's drome. *That was brilliant,* she thought. *Out of this world!*

Zut had been working on the computer program to destroy the Hologram Shrine when she appeared in front of him, but he'd instantly stopped working, got up and held her shoulders firmly. Then he kissed the top of her head and said how proud he was of her. He'd beckoned for her to sit down and told her how incredibly clever she was to find the hidden robot lens. He thought that he'd hidden it really well for the last thirty years. Pren, the last person to find it, was now captain of the Searchers.

Ashtez's eyes had lit up as he mentioned "Searchers." Dare she mention that was her ambition? Before she could pluck up courage to say anything, Zut was telling her that he would remember her name because when she was due to leave cerebrumadrome and join the Planet Force there would be a position free for a Searcher, as that was the day one of the present Searchers became a wizend.

Ashtez hoped that Zut hadn't noticed the tears in her eyes. She was so happy that her eyes were filling up with emotion. Their leader must not see them; he would think her weak and weak people did not make Searchers. Quickly she took her gaming lens out and pretended to clean it so that he would think there was some dust making her eyes water. She put it back in and with a big smile thanked Zut, telling him it was her greatest ambition to be a Searcher and she hoped when she left cerebrumadrome she would be worthy to join the Searchers.

Zut nodded and then Ashtez found herself being teleported once again and sitting on the flier next to Hurlen. Thankfully he was busy gaming, so didn't notice her arrive. She wanted to sit and bask in her glory all on her own. Her brain had taken over and she was visualising finding life forms as a Searcher, when to her annoyance she was teleported and inside the wizend's drome, being handed one of those disgusting mince pies!

Odraine hugged Ashtez so tightly she could barely breathe, but she didn't mind. She realized he was so full of pride and emotion and that he couldn't speak. Words were inadequate at a time like this, though.

"I've just realized," said Odraine, "you've not only found and beaten the hidden robot lens, but you're the first female ever to do so. This is just incredible."

Ashtez grinned. She'd forgotten she was the first female ever to win. Finding and beating the hidden robot lens had been her ultimate goal for ages, so that Zut would notice her and would remember her name when she applied to be a Searcher.

"I think my daughter and I should got to the Galiquer for a few galiquons to celebrate, don't you?" he said, beaming.

Ashtez couldn't believe her ears. Her father was actually taking her to the Galiquer for a few galiquons. This was unbelievable. Normally the Galiquer was divided into children, adults and wizends and they never mixed. It was such an honour to be invited into the adult drome.

Odraine set the panel on the teleport tube. Normally he would jump on the flier to go to the Galiquer, but this was a very special occasion. His daughter was the first female ever to find and beat the hidden gaming lens. Only the best transport was good enough for his daughter.

Ashtez found herself surrounded by adults, but they didn't seem to mind that a child was in their section. In fact, she was being welcomed by everyone and had straws and straws of galiquons lined up in front of her. It was such a rare event. In fact, it was a miracle and everyone wanted to celebrate it.

Sirleen the Spirit Master bought a double galiquon and placed it in front of Ashtez. "Congratulations, Ashtez. We are all very proud of you. I've just seen the battle you had to find that hidden robot lens on the Tirleen data," he said, smiling at her and raised his straw to toast her. "I think we have a future Searcher here, don't you? Anyone who can fight a battle like that and win deserves the honour of being a Searcher."

Everyone agreed with Sirleen and raised their straws as they toasted Ashtez. The cheering reached the children's and wizend's section and soon the whole Galiquon was ringing with praises for her as they all joined in. Ashtez's ears were buzzing with the noise and she grinned from ear to ear. This would definitely be something to tell her friends about tomorrow, she thought as she swallowed another galiquon. Her head was spinning and she would have a thumping headache when she woke up, but she didn't care. The Spirit Master had toasted her and kept calling her his little miracle. She wasn't so sure about miracle. It was her brains and knowledge of wires that had helped her win. No miracle was involved here.

Sirleen felt happy. Yes, he had drunk several galiquons and the room was spinning, but he'd finally found out what this miracle was. Someone finding the hidden robot lens and a female at that. He sat and smiled to himself, and in his stupefied state didn't even realize that if this was the miracle, then there must be a God to make it!

Chapter 4

God's Gifts

Viola sat in front of the hologram of her beloved daughter, Anjoy. She was now twelve years old and very beautiful. Her long blonde hair shone in the light and Viola imagined what it would be like to brush it every night. Tears formed in her eyes as she realized she would never see her again after today. Why was Zut destroying the shrine? Didn't he realize the comfort it gave her and the twenty-four other parents whose babies had been stillborn. She put her hand through the hologram and tried to feel Anjoy. Oh, if only she could touch her, stroke her face, kiss her, anything, even if it was only for a minute.

Her mind wandered back to Anjoy's birth twelve years ago. It was unheard of to lose a baby. Everything was followed meticulously. Women or men were not allowed to get pregnant before the age of fifty because they weren't considered mature enough to handle it before then. Plus, from the ages twenty-five to fifty everybody had to serve in the Planet Force. Up until then their brains were energized with information every day for sixty wixons. By the time they were twenty-five they knew everything anyone could possibly ever want to know.

She was very proud when she was chosen to provide the main gene to create their first child. The pregnancy had been scanned and accelerated daily for the normal nine days and as usual there were no problems. It was only when they used the introducing wire that introduced the baby to the Transfer Room, where they inserted the wires needed to receive all the knowledge obtained from cerebrumadrome, that they realized that she was dead. Pandemonium had followed in the Transfer Room. They had never known it to happen before, but then it happened to twenty-four other people.

Finally, when answers were demanded from those people that had been chosen next to create life, they found a minute fault in the acceleration process that only occurred in every tenth baby. It was accelerating the heart growth so fast that it aged it to two hundred and fifty years, meaning the heart was dead before the baby was even born.

She remembered the aftermath of their daughter's death. The wizend told them it was God punishing them for not believing in him and not being registered. Viola had even attended a few secret Faith meetings and in her distress was starting to believe her. Then they had a personal visit from their leader, who told them that was utter nonsense. God didn't exist. They asked if they could register as partners earlier than the normal age of seventy-five. They didn't tell their leader, but hoped this would appease God and that he would let them keep their next child. Their leader wouldn't hear of it. Far too young, he'd said. Once their first child started Planet Force that would be early enough. They only had twenty-five years to wait, so why were they being so impatient?

Viola wiped the tears away that were running down her face and prepared to switch the hologram off. She only had fifteen wixes of her visiting time left anyhow and she wanted to look at her daughter's smiling face without it being blurred by the tears. She wished Odraine had come with her to say goodbye, but he had said he couldn't bear it, knowing that when they switched off the Hologram Shrine today, that would be it. No more Anjoy.

They had never experienced the emotion of death before because it was accepted that everyone died at two hundred and fifty years. The night before the wizend went to the Farewell Room to die and their remains evaporated, everyone went to the Galiquer and had so many galiquons they could barely remember what the wizend looked like when they surfaced in the morning. Illness and accidents did not exist on Planet Tirleen. They had seen pictures of such things on their lens at cerebrumadrome from a thousand years ago, but now in the year 3030 transport was safe and no one became ill.

She wiped her face again as more tears poured down while she prepared to switch the hologram off. She blinked as she looked at Anjoy. Her mind must be playing tricks with her. She could have sworn that her daughter had waved at her. She smiled at Anjoy and waved back, realizing that Zut had probably programmed it into the hologram as a farewell present for them.

With a very heavy heart Viola switched the hologram off as the light came on to signal the end of visiting. She didn't want the Guardians doing it for her, which they would do if she didn't obey Zut's orders and do it herself. The hologram of Anjoy faded and the tube went blank. Viola closed her eyes. She couldn't bear to see her daughter disappear. She was aware of some of the other parents screaming, but she was going to try and remain composed. Emotion was frowned on by Zut and she didn't want to be in trouble.

She wiped her face yet again so that she could see clearly to leave the Hologram Shrine and then bravely opened her eyes, preparing herself to look at the blank tube. The screaming in her ears echoed and she realized it was coming from her throat. Stood in front of the tube was her beloved daughter, Anjoy. She was smiling at her and SHE WAS ALIVE!

Chapter 5
Too Many Galiquons?

Sirleen switched the Tirleen data off. Ashtez was certainly the hero of their planet. Every ten minutes the data was updated, but Ashtez still remained at the top of all the data. It was so incredible that someone had actually found the hidden robot lens, and a female at that. He'd heard that Pren, the last person to find the hidden robot lens, had been informed. He was on a spaceship somewhere looking for "life," but the news had been relayed to him as it was so important. Apparently he was furious that someone now held his title of "Wiron Leader," she was a female, and she was also in line to be a Searcher. He, as captain of the Searchers, did not want somebody who had taken his title away from him on his team.

Sirleen hoped Pren didn't come back and stir trouble up for Ashtez, because he liked her and she was his "miracle." He'd heard that Viola's wizend was attending secret Faith meetings and was hoping to see her in secret and tell her to stop all this nonsense as it could affect Ashtez becoming a Searcher. If Pren came back and found out, he would let Zut know and Edril would be captured and put on public display in a living tube until she died. Zut would never forgive anyone connected with her, so finding and beating the hidden robot lens or not, Ashtez's dream of being a Searcher would be finished.

He was glad the miracle had finally happened. Now he'd stopped eating those disgusting mince pies the nightmares had gone, and of course the miracle had happened and obviously his job was to help protect Ashtez from Pren causing any trouble.

It was weird how he'd started dreaming, though. The analysis of the mince pies hadn't come up with anything except that they were full of glycogen, which he supposed accelerated the brain waves. Obviously that was why he'd been able to start dreaming. It was funny how no one else had complained of having dreams at Giving time, though. Perhaps it was just because he was more susceptible to the mince pies than they were.

It had been a bit worrying that the Spirit Master had been getting messages from God. He laughed as he remembered the vision of the angel at the end of his bed. It was the sort of thing that you could visualise after too many galiquons, which he'd had earlier as they all toasted Ashtez. His head was a bit blurry at the moment, but he had to update the data on "why the birth of Jesus was just a fairy tale" for the cerebrumadrome tomorrow.

He switched the screen on and started to add to the program. Coincidentally it was the picture of the angel telling the shepherds of great news. He laughed and started to add why this was all rubbish, and at the same time wiping the picture of the angel away, because apart from him and Zut no one was allowed to see any of these fairy tale pictures in case it influenced their minds. Zut was sure the Faith Believers had found some pictures of angels and stories of this God and that was why they believed in the fairy tales.

As soon as he deleted the picture of the angel, another angel appeared. Sirleen was annoyed. How had that happened? He tried to delete the picture, but the angel on the screen became bigger until just her face was on the screen. Sirleen frantically pressed buttons. What was wrong with the program? This shouldn't happen. He switched the program off and then on again and screamed out when not only was the angel's face still there, but it was now speaking to him.

"Sirleen, don't do that again. You must listen to me. You are..."

The angel got no further, as Sirleen hastily switched the screen off. He was sweating. "Too many galiquons, too many galiquons," he said aloud. "Too many galiquons, never again."

He was just deciding whether to risk turning the screen back on or not when a message came over his intercom.

"Spirit Master to our leader's drome *immediately*," yelled a voice.

Sirleen jumped as the voice screamed the last word. Whatever was wrong? He hoped no one had found out that Viola's wizend was a Faith Believer and had reported her to Zut. He desperately wanted to get to her first and tell her she must not attend any more meetings.

Forgetting about his blurry headache and seeing the angel speak to him, Sirleen pressed the teleport switch and in a second found himself staring into Zut's very angry face.

Chapter 6
Drome Arrest

Odraine hugged Ashtez tightly. She was shaking with fear. So was he, if it was known, but he couldn't let her see that. They were surrounded by the Planet Force guards, who'd suddenly appeared from the teleport in front of them. They had only been back from the Galiquer a few minutes and were both feeling a little wobbly from all the galiquons. They had hoped Viola would be back so that they could tell her Ashtez's fantastic news, but instead here was the Planet Force guards telling them they were under drome arrest.

Ashtez was scared and at the same time very angry. *That stupid wizend had been caught,* she thought. Now any hopes of being a Searcher had gone for ever. How she hated her. All that planning and effort into finding and beating the hidden robot lens had been for nothing, and all because that stupid wizend was attending meetings about someone who never existed.

"Dad, Dad, tell them they've brainwashed the wizend, she doesn't know what she's doing. It's because she's so old she doesn't know what she's doing. Please, Dad, please tell them she's been brainwashed," she frantically begged him.

Odraine looked at his daughter's frantic face. Of course, that was it. The stupid wizend had been caught. All that celebrating Ashtez's success was for nothing now. Zut would never let her be a Searcher now they'd caught Edril. Damn her. He must try to do something to help save Ashtez's future career.

"Captain Braze, I beg of you to let me explain. She has been brainwashed, she can't help what she's doing. Please release us," he desperately begged as he looked into Captain Braze's stern face.

"Viola's been brainwashed? By whom? Who has brainwashed her? Tell me at once and I will relay the message to Zut," Captain Braze commanded.

"Viola?" gasped Odraine in shock. Oh no! Surely she hadn't gone straight from the Hologram Shrine to a secret Faith meeting? That stupid wizend had obviously told her it was all her fault Anjoy died because she wasn't a Believer. *What a mess,* he thought. Now what could he do? How was he going to save Viola and help the rest of his family?

Ashtez looked at her father in shock and horror. "Mum? They've brainwashed her, Dad. What are we going to do?"

Captain Braze looked puzzled. Viola, brainwashed? What on earth were they on about? Were they suggesting that Zut's hologram program had brainwashed Viola? Zut would be very angry if he heard that. He'd been trying to help the families get over their babies' deaths and here was one of the relatives suggesting that Zut was brainwashing them.

Yes, maybe something had gone wrong with the program, as when the holograms were switched off the children were still there, but in some sort of solid matter and seemed to be actually breathing and telling their parents that they were alive. They were even suggesting that God had sent them as a miracle to make people believe once again. God indeed! He laughed at the thought of an invisible man, who didn't exist anyhow, sending these dead children back to life. He didn't know what was going on, but they obviously weren't really alive. It was some sort of trick. Someone had somehow got into the hologram program and tampered with it.

Zut was furious and until he'd found out who had done it, the Hologram Shrine was locked with the parents and "things" in it and the rest of the families were under drome arrest. One of these families was the culprit. They were obviously annoyed at Zut for going to destroy the Hologram Shrine so were getting their own back.

Well, it wouldn't work, he thought. They would soon catch the person responsible, then they would suffer. He'd never seen Zut so angry. Mind you, when the culprit was found, they and their families deserved everything they got. How dare they suggest the children were sent from this man God. Zut was sure the Faith Believers were behind this, so that meant someone in one of the children's families was a Faith Believer. Well, they'd soon find out that being locked in a sealed living tube on public display until they were two hundred and fifty years old was no joke.

Captain Braze looked at Odraine and wondered if he was the culprit. He'd just mentioned that Viola was brainwashed, so who'd brainwashed her?

"Has Viola been attending secret Faith meetings?" he said sternly to Odraine.

"No, no, of course she hasn't. We hate the Faith Believers. Don't we, Ashtez?" he said, hoping he sounded convincing. He wasn't sure if Viola had attended any secret Faith meetings, but Edril, her wizend, had been pushing her to. He knew that much.

"No, Captain Braze, Mum has never been to a secret Faith meeting. We really hate Faith Believers. Ask dad's wizends, they'll tell you how much we hate them," she said desperately. *That was the answer,* she thought. Dad's wizends would help them. They hated Faith Believers, so would back them up.

Captain Braze looked at their desperate faces and thought about it. They could be innocent, but then Ashtez had used her knowledge of wires to find and beat the hidden gaming lens. That was unheard of, so perhaps she'd found a way to tamper with the program.

"When did you last visit your sister?" he said, pointing a finger at Ashtez.

"Me?" She was quaking with fear. "I don't have a sister and as for visiting that creepy image, you must be joking. I've never been to the Hologram Shrine. What's the point? Dead is dead. I've never had a sister, just my brother, Hurlen."

She hoped she'd sounded disgusted at the thought of visiting the shrine and that Captain Braze had believed her. Whatever was happening and what on earth did that dead thing have to do with it? She hoped her mother hadn't got so emotional when the hologram was turned off and did or even said something stupid. Zut didn't like emotion. If Captain Braze was asking questions about the Hologram Shrine then something must have happened there.

Oh no! Surely Zut hadn't destroyed it with the parents inside, she thought. But then why was he asking when she'd last visited it? It had to center around the Hologram Shrine, so perhaps something went wrong with the program when they switched it off for the last time and the image remained instead of disappearing.

She wished she knew; her whole future as a Searcher was at stake here and at this moment it was very difficult to stand, let alone think after all the galiquons they'd consumed. She needed her brain to be alert to answer Captain Braze's questions. One wrong answer and they were in serious trouble.

Chapter 7
Zut Meets the Programs

Sirleen tried to take in what Zut was saying, but he was so angry he was screaming the words out and Sirleen could barely make out what he was on about.

"They've vandalized the program," Zut screamed as he paced up and down the room.

"What program?" said Sirleen, very puzzled. Why on earth had he been summoned, and immediately at that, just because a program had been tampered with?

"The Hologram Shrine, it's been tampered with," Zut yelled again.

Sirleen was very confused. Had someone found a way to stop the Hologram Shrine from turning off? If so, why?

"I'm sorry, Zut, but I don't understand. You're not making any sense."

"Come with me," said Zut.

He pulled Sirleen to the teleport and in a few seconds Sirleen found himself in the Hologram Shrine.

It was pandemonium! The parents of the dead children were screaming in what appeared to be joy and by their sides stood some sort of solid image of their child.

"Look at this, look at this," screamed Zut, who was now very red in the face. "Can't you see they've done something? The images remain, only they're solid."

Sirleen looked at the children as their parents hugged and wept over them. They certainly looked real. In fact they looked as if they were alive. Whoever had tampered with the program was very good indeed. Ashtez! The name immediately came into his head. Oh no! Surely she wouldn't do anything so stupid? Surely she wouldn't ruin her chances of being a Searcher to do something as stupid as this? No, of course she wouldn't. Someone else was behind this.

Anjoy walked up to the Spirit Master and took his hand. He gasped in surprise and a little fear as well. This "thing" felt real. It was very creepy indeed. He didn't like this at all. A vision of the angel's face kept coming into his mind and her voice was saying to listen. Then he had a flashback to all those nightmares and the angel saying a "miracle" was going to happen. Surely this couldn't be the miracle? No, no, of course it couldn't. How could it? God didn't exist. He shook his head to try and push the vision from his mind. Whoever had tampered with the program had made a really good job of it. These "things" felt very real indeed. Much too real for his liking. He let go of Anjoy's hand quickly.

"This, this is what is wrong," yelled Zut as he prodded Anjoy on the chest.

Zut recoiled in horror as he touched Anjoy. It was so horrible; that "thing" actually felt real. How on earth had they done it? Somebody was very, very clever. Much too clever for his liking. He couldn't have someone cleverer than himself, for they could take over the entire planet and change people's minds.

Anjoy tried to pick Sirleen's hand up once again to get his attention, but no sooner had she touched him than he also recoiled in horror.

"This is terrible, absolutely terrible. Zut, what on earth has happened? You were destroying the shrine today. What's gone wrong?" said Sirleen, wishing that the "thing" would move away from him and stop staring at him in the face.

"Great Spirit Master, you have to help us," said Anjoy as Sirleen started to back away from her.

"Me, help?" he gasped. He didn't know if he was more amazed at the fact that this "thing" could speak, or that it was asking him for his help. He looked at Zut in disbelief. "It just spoke to me," Sirleen said, shaking with fear.

"Don't panic. Whoever has done this has just added a program to help them speak," said Zut, who had now got over the shock of seeing these "things" in place of the holograms and was looking at them more closely.

Zut pulled Anjoy closer to himself and felt her body and her hair and prodded her head. It felt like she had brains in there. *That was very, very clever,* he thought. He was now actually quite impressed with these "things." It took a very clever mind indeed to write a program to do this. He pinched Anjoy's cheek to feel for the metal wiring underneath, but none seemed to be there.

"Ouch!" Anjoy screamed at the pain Zut was causing her. God hadn't told her that people were going to hurt her, only that the Spirit Master would help them. They knew they had a hard task ahead of them to try and change all the bad ways on the planet and tell them about God. But pain, no, he hadn't mentioned anything about pain.

She wasn't sure she was so happy about coming back to life again now. All she'd ever known was heaven and she'd enjoyed being there. It was such a peaceful and happy place with no pain. Definitely no pain. She thought she would be glad to live with her family again and was looking forward to hugging and kissing her mother, who'd devotedly visited her every week at the shrine. She'd stood behind and watched her pouring her feelings and emotion out to this hologram and wishing her mother could actually feel when she touched her and answered her back.

When God had summoned all the children together and said he wanted them to help him with a miracle that would bring great joy to the planet Tirleen once again, they were all very excited. He explained that he was sending them back to live with their families and they would experience love, joy, excitement, but also disbelief and anger, as there were a lot of people on this planet who did not believe in him.

The children found this hard to believe. Why didn't these people believe in this wonderful man? Because he was wonderful, very wonderful, full of love and kindness. He explained that as well as not believing in him, some of these people were also behaving very badly indeed. Young children were allowed to drink and get drunk, and those people that followed God's ways were not allowed to openly pray to him, but had to hold secret meetings. If they were caught they were imprisoned in tubes and put on public display to deter any other people from believing in him.

Their task was to try and free the people who were believers and to show everyone that not only did God exist, but that he was a kind and loving man. They also had to try and get people to change their ways and be good and kind. If they could get the Faith Believers released and allowed to worship God openly, then they would help them and soon everyone would realize that God did exist and that he was kind and loving. However, if they kept on denying him, then God would be very angry indeed and they would feel his wrath.

"Wonderful, they feel pain as well," Zut said, laughing as Anjoy yelled.

He opened her mouth and prodded around her teeth. Anjoy thought this was disgusting, so she closed her mouth and clamped her teeth down hard on Zut's finger.

Zut screamed in agony and tried to force Anjoy to open her mouth by pressing his other hand on her face, but Anjoy just clamped harder on the finger.

"Stop her, stop her," Zut yelled to Sirleen.

Sirleen was panicking. Somehow these "things" were attacking their leader. He put a hand on her jaw and one on her lip and forced her mouth open. Zut quickly pulled his finger out and held it tightly in the other hand to ease the throbbing pain.

"They've been programmed to attack us," Zut said in horror. "We must find out how to destroy then before they take us over."

Anjoy grimaced at the taste left in her mouth by Zut's finger.

"I hope your hands were clean! Cleanliness is next to Godliness, you know," she said to Zut, who gasped as the word God was mentioned.

"This is terrible. It's much, much worse than I thought. As well as being programmed to attack us, they've been programmed to talk as if this God man exists," Zut exclaimed.

"God told us that you would help us in our task, Spirit Master," said Anjoy, pulling on Sirleen's arm to get his attention again.

His nightmare was coming back to haunt him, Sirleen thought. Perhaps it wasn't those mince pies; perhaps too much galiquons caused hallucinations? He had seen the angel's face grow and talk to him on the screen when he had just come back from the Galiquer. God didn't exist. How could he help if he didn't exist and anyhow, how could he help something that had only been programmed to live?

"Ignore her, Sirleen, and whatever you do, don't look into her eyes. They've probably been programmed to hypnotize us into believing them about this God," said Zut, deliberately ignoring Anjoy's eyes.

He had seen how bright and sparkly they were, and when they stared at you it was as if they were looking right into your brain cells. It was very scary. If they weren't careful these children would soon have the whole planet hypnotized and whoever had tampered with the program would be running the planet instead of him.

Zut pushed Anjoy backward to move her out of his way and avoid her staring at them. Anjoy yelled out in agony as she fell on the floor and hit her bottom hard. More pain and they'd only been alive for a short time! She hoped there wasn't going to be a lot of this pain and wished she could talk to God to ask him how to avoid it. Tears came into her eyes and then ran down her face, wetting it. She put her hand up to wipe them away and wondered what was happening. Why was her face wet? This had never happened in heaven. How she wished she could ask God all of these questions and feel his arms comforting her again. As the tears poured down her face Viola ran up and comforted her.

"Leave her alone," she screamed at Zut and advanced on him with such speed that he was completely taken unaware when she struck him hard on the face.

Zut gasped in shock and pain. He'd never been struck before. He was their leader and no one had ever dared to touch him.

Sirleen watched as Zut's face got redder and redder, partly from the attack and partly from anger and frustration. He felt he ought to do something, but what? The children almost seemed to be in control here. Their parents were obviously under their power and had been commanded to attack anyone who approached them. It obviously wasn't Viola's fault; she was a quiet, placid woman, yet here she was acting like one of the cave women he'd seen on old memory data, protecting their young.

Zut tried to think. His brain cells were almost popping with anger, but he had to use them wisely to work out what to do in this situation. They were only women and children, and not really children at that, just programs, but dare he risk arresting them all? Perhaps he ought to check with the Planet Force guards first and see if they'd found out anything from the families of these "things." That was probably the best idea, then he could sit quietly and think how to break this program and self-destruct all these beings.

He spoke to Bence, the leader of the Guardians, who stood well away from any of the children. Bence wasn't too sure what was happening here and was hoping that Zut would sort it out. It had been a big surprise to him and the other Guardians when the holograms had been switched off. He had been expecting something from the parents, but when the screaming had started it had panicked him. The emotion from all the parents was very scary, and he was trying to think how to deal with it when he realized why they were all screaming. It wasn't through sorrow, but joy!

The other Guardians had been just as scared and had rushed up to him demanding to know what to do and asking where these "things" had appeared from? He ordered them to double check that they had turned the hologram program off. When they came back and confirmed it was off, he had made them check it again. He was certain they must have missed something, otherwise why had this happened? It was when they all confirmed that the program had definitely been turned off and there was no way it could still be working that he had started to panic.

He knew that Zut would blame them for this and say they'd switched the program off incorrectly. He had looked at the children again to make sure he wasn't imagining things. They certainly looked real. Too real and solid for holograms. Their parents were able to hug and kiss them and their hands didn't go through their bodies.

Whatever was happening was certainly very clever. Then it struck him! This was something that Zut had programmed into the hologram so that when the program was switched off these "things" remained for a short time to allow their parents to feel them and then they would disappear before he destroyed the whole Hologram Shrine.

He had told the other Guardians what Zut had probably done and they were to stop panicking, these "things" would disappear soon. Bence had wished their leader had told them he'd put this in the program. He didn't like to be taken unaware of anything. He was in charge of the shrine and it made him look stupid if he started panicking about something. What was their leader trying to do? Scare them? Zut wasn't the sort of person who played practical jokes. In fact, he hated emotion of any sort, so this was all very odd.

He felt very annoyed that Zut had not bothered to inform him of this ending to the program. They would have known how to deal with the parents' emotions if they'd been told and could then have dealt with the situation. Instead, they were all made to look stupid as these "things" appeared and they'd looked on helplessly not knowing if they should be doing something or not.

The Guardians had all waited for the "things" to disappear. They waited and waited, but the "things" remained. Bence wondered how long Zut had programmed these "things" to be there. The parents were all demanding to leave and take their children home with them. They didn't seem to realize that these "things" weren't real and would disappear soon. It had all gotten very difficult the longer those "things" remained. The more the parents thought they were real, the more they started to get annoyed with the Guardians for not allowing them to take their children home.

It was when one of the children, who her parents had named Anjoy, approached him and said they were real and that God had sent them back that he started to get twitchy and nervous. He knew Zut would never program anything to speak of God. That person didn't exist. It was then that Bence had sent a message to Zut to see if he knew what was happening. From Zut's reaction he knew this wasn't meant to happen. He was very relieved when Zut had appeared with Sirleen. It was their problem now. They could deal with it!

"Send a message to the Planet Force headquarters to double the guards outside the Hologram Shrine. Sirleen and I will go to my quarters and decide what to do with this problem," Zut said to Bence.

Bence didn't know whether to be pleased or not. On the one hand there would be plenty of guards outside the shrine to stop these "things" from leaving with their parents, but on the other, he thought, they would be alone in the shrine with these "things" and if anything happened would the guards be able to help them in time if they were outside?

Once he was sure the Hologram Shrine was securely protected by the Planet Force guards, Zut left with Sirleen. He wasn't too sure if doubling the guards would be enough. These "things" were very clever. Would they find a way to get out of the Hologram Shrine, or would they be able to overpower the Planet Force guards somehow?

The Planet Force guards and the Guardians were all given strict instructions that on no account were they to look into these things' eyes. They were very powerful and would hypnotize them. Then they would be able to command them to do whatever they wished.

The Guardians stared straight ahead, avoiding the children and their parents' eyes as they were left alone. Now their leader had gone and they were alone with these "things." They were all very scared. What should they do if they were approached by one of them? The Planet Force guards were outside the shrine, not in. Bence tried to remain calm, the other Guardians must not realize how scared he was. He wondered if he dared ask some of the Planet Force guards to come inside and protect them, but then decided against it. Zut was very angry at the moment and any form of disobedience, however small, would be dealt with very severely. Perhaps Zut would start putting anyone who annoyed him in a living tube along with the Faith Believers. He shuddered at the thought of it. No, if he just stared straight ahead then he was sure they would all be safe from these "things."

Chapter 8
Testing Their Faith

Edril stared and stared, not sure whether to believe her eyes or not. Yes, the reason she attended these secret Faith meetings was because she believed that God did exist and would one day come back to help save their planet and get rid of all that was bad on it. At the moment, however, she wasn't sure if her eyes were playing tricks on her, or if that small amount of galiquon she'd consumed as she'd taken the faith once again had gone to her head and she was hallucinating. But then everyone else in the tunnel were rubbing and blinking their eyes as if they could see the same thing as her.

Zincon, leader of the Faith Believers, was at the front of the tunnel on his knees and shielding his eyes from the bright light. He wondered if he was being tested by God. Of course he believed in him, he was the leader of the Faith Believers after all, but was this apparition in front of him an angel or not?

He knew they existed and even though Sirleen had done his best to erase all data on angels from the planet's library, Faith Believers from the past had managed to steal some data that had pictures and stories about angels. They had handed them down through the generations so it could be proved that they did exist.

They were well hidden, but he'd been privileged to see the information, so knew what an angel looked like. In fact, like this one in front of him! *It must be an angel,* he thought. Why else was it so bright that his eyes could barely look at it?

"Be careful, Zincon, it may be a trick," shouted Kalsi, who was knelt behind him. She had felt very uneasy when this bright light had appeared and now it seemed to be hovering above them.

Zincon thought about this. Kalsi may be right. Now he was really worried. Perhaps Zut knew about this tunnel and had hidden a program somewhere to beam this light down with an apparition of an angel in it. Then when they were all blinded by the light, the Planet Force guards would rush in and capture them and imprison them all in living tubes. It was a horrifying thought and now Zincon was terrified. He jumped up and was just going to tell everyone to flee and hide when the angel spoke.

"Fear not, Faith Believers. God has sent me to tell you that a miracle has happened on your planet and you must help with it. Sirleen has been approached and will also help in this great task. Be prepared, all of you, and be brave."

The angel and its bright light disappeared.

Zincon looked at the other Faith Believers. Some were already leaving in a desperate hurry to hide somewhere. Like him they'd obviously come to the same conclusion. Zut had made one mistake with this program. He'd mentioned that Sirleen would help them. Everyone in this room knew that Sirleen, the Spirit Master, would never help people to believe in God. His job was to make sure they knew he didn't exist.

"Everybody go home as quickly as possible. Make sure you are not seen leaving this tunnel. I will find somewhere different for the next meeting and get a message to you all. Oh, and make sure you all have an alibi for tonight," Zincon shouted, suddenly remembering to add this last bit. If anyone was questioned about tonight they would need to provide a watertight alibi, otherwise Zut's suspicions would be raised and if one Faith Believer was caught, it could snowball and they may all be found out and put on display in those awful living tubes.

Zincon picked all the empty straws of galiquon up off the floor and put them in his pocket, along with the piece of paper with his Belief notes on. He would sneak them into the evaporator at work tomorrow when no one was looking. That was one good think about working in the Evaporation Room. He was able to evaporate all evidence from their meetings. If any of their tunnels were found and searched, then something as small as one of these straws could provide the evidence needed by the Planet Force guards to arrest them. They would use them to get samples from and match them on the Planet's mitosis data, then they would know who had been using the tunnel, and alibi's or not, they would arrest them.

After Zut's attempt to fool them today, though, he must take even more care than normal. Especially in the Evaporation Room. Furnise, the chief controller of the Evaporation Room, was starting to get a bit suspicious of him. Zincon could easily hide the notes and straws on one of the wizend's due for evaporation, but he would have to take extra care when he gave them a blessing before they went into the Evaporator. Most of them were not Faith Believers, but he felt he owed it to them to give them a final blessing before they went. He knew that once they'd died they would get the shock of their lives when they found themselves staring into the face of God in heaven!

He had managed to convince Furnise that he was just saying, "Hope you had a good life" to them, but Furnise was starting to question why he felt he had to do this.

Now he blessed them silently in his mind and hoped that was good enough. God heard you wherever you were, so he must be able to read minds.

Zincon checked that no evidence of their meeting was left anywhere in the tunnel and cautiously and very nervously looked out at the entrance to see if he was being watched. Satisfied he wasn't, or that none of the Planet Force guards were anywhere around, he hurriedly left to go home.

All the way home he was praying for the parents of the children who had died and were visiting the Hologram Shrine for the last time today. He was one of the lucky ones, as their child was created at the same time, but luckily Carik had lived. He thanked God for it every day whilst he also prayed for those children who had died.

It was very cruel of Zut to turn the holograms off. How were these parents going to cope? No one had ever lost a baby or child before, and at least these holograms gave them some comfort. Zut obviously felt that he didn't need to ease his conscience any longer and wasn't worried how the parents would feel when the Hologram Shrine was destroyed.

Zincon decided to change direction. He was just passing a flier entrance and caught a flier to Odraine and Viola's drome. *They would probably need some comforting,* he thought. Odraine didn't know he was a Faith Believer, but Viola had attended a few secret meetings with her wizend, Edril, so she knew but would keep it a secret.

Zincon was teleported outside Odraine and Viola's drome, but before the flier moved off again he promptly pressed the teleport button and to his relief found himself back on the flier. He was trembling and beads of perspiration were running down his forehead.

The drome was surrounded by the Planet Force guards. Had they found out that Edril was a Faith Believer and that Viola had attended a few meetings? He hoped not, because Viola could be in such a distressed state after leaving the Hologram Shrine that she may let slip that he was the leader of the Faith Believers and then they would be after him. As the flier flew off he kept looking out of the portholes to check that it wasn't being chased by the Planet Force guards. So far he was safe; the only other transport in the air was the other fliers. Perhaps he ought to go into hiding for a while, but then if he didn't turn up at the Evaporation Room in the morning that could arouse suspicion.

He couldn't understand why their house was surrounded by the Planet Force guards, though. If they suspected someone was a Faith Believer they would normally just arrest them and take them straight to the Forcedrome for questioning. What was going on? *Wait a minute,* he suddenly thought. What an idiot he'd been in panicking. Ashtez had just become the new Wiron Leader, the first one in many years and the very first female ever. He'd heard this astonishing information on the Tirleen data before he'd left for the meeting.

Of course they were probably giving her an escort to some special ceremony or something. He felt very silly now, panicking at the sight of the Planet Force guards. He hoped they hadn't seen him teleport off the flier and then straight back on. It would look very suspicious and they might question what he was up to.

As the flier flew over the Hologram Shrine, the inside became full of the sound of noisy chattering. Zincon wondered what all the fuss was. He heard the words "Planet Force guards" and quickly looked out of the porthole; perhaps they were chasing him after all. No, there weren't any following the flier. He looked down and, to his amazement, saw that not only was the Hologram Shrine still there and not destroyed by Zut, but it was surrounded by many of the Planet Force guards. Quite a lot, in fact.

Something was going on, but what? It must be something to do with the hologram program because the Planet Force guards were surrounding Odraine and Viola's drome as well, and their daughter was one of the babies that had died. He hoped Viola and the other parents hadn't become so hysterical when the holograms were switched off that they'd attacked the guardians. He could understand how upset they would be, but Zut would never tolerate the guardians being attacked. He wondered how he could find out what was going on.

"Several of the other dromes were surrounded by the Planet Force guards."

Zincon's ears pricked up as he heard the person opposite him say this. What other dromes were they on about? He hoped it wasn't the Faith Believers' dromes. He must try to find out.

"Excuse me, I notice there seem to be a lot of Planet Force guards around places today. Do you know what is going on?" he said, trying to sound casual and as though he was just passing the time of day with the person opposite him.

"All the dromes that have been surrounded by the Planet Force guards are of the hologram children. The shrine was supposed to be destroyed today, you know."

The man was as anxious as Zincon to find out what was going on as well. It was very unsettling with the Planet Force guards everywhere, looking as if they were going to arrest people. He was on his way to the Galiquer, where he intended to stay and drink galiquons, all night if necessary, until he felt it was safe to go home.

"I thought the Hologram Shrine was going to be destroyed today, but it still appears to be here. I wonder what is going on?" said Zincon.

"I don't know, but one of the controllers who works in our leader's drome let slip to a friend of mine that Zut was in a furious temper. Apparently he had been summoned to the Hologram Shrine by the leader of the guardians, and he'd returned with the Spirit Master later and they both looked very worried and angry."

Hearing this information at least gave Zincon some relief. Now he knew that the Planet Force guards were not after him he could relax for a while. Zut had obviously been too busy dealing with the problem at the Hologram Shrine to capture them at the meeting earlier, but he was obviously on to them or why else would he have put that illusion in the tunnel? He wondered how Zut had got the information on an angel to program one to appear at their meeting. He hoped their hidden data on angels was still safe and that Zut hadn't found it. Only he as the leader of the Faith Believers knew where it was, and he thought it was really well hidden.

Surely Zut would not be able to find it? How did Zut know what an angel looked like, though? Perhaps Sirleen as the Spirit Master still had some data on angels. Nobody had ever seen one on the data he programmed for them at cerebrumadrome, but then Sirleen was always surprising them with new data as to why God didn't exist, so perhaps he did have some images of angels and he'd let Zut have them.

Sirleen would certainly have a shock when he died. He wondered how he was going to explain to God when he met him that he didn't exist? Zincon would love to be in heaven when Zut died, but as he was only sixty-two years old and Sirleen sixty-five years old, he would have a few years to wait to find out what God did say to him!

Most of the Faith Believers were wizends and well into their one or two hundredth year, but he was very young to be a Faith Believer and the leader at that. It was the reason he felt that he was quite safe and that Zut would never find out about him. When their last leader had gone to the Evaporation Room it had been decided to elect him as the new leader because he was so young and would arouse less suspicion when he organized meetings.

Despite being told by Sirleen at cerebrumadrome that God did not exist and Zincon's wizends hating Faith Believers, he always felt deep inside him that someone must have created all these worlds. Even if there was only their planet left because of all the wars, then who created it in the first place?

He remembered finding out where one of the secret meetings was going to be held and attending his first one. He was scared stiff of being found out, both by the Planet Force guards and his wizends. They would never accept him as their son if they knew he was at a meeting. When he had listened to the words spoken by the previous leader of the Faith Believers, he knew he was right. These people felt the same way he did. God did exist, and when you died you weren't a nothing, but lived in heaven with God, or were reborn again.

From then on he became a Faith Believer and attended as many secret meetings as he could. Like the others, he was terrified when Zut started capturing some of them and imprisoning them in living tubes and putting them on public display. It was awful passing them every day; they were all his friends and to watch them in their living hell was horrendous. Some of the Faith Believers had become so scared of being caught and imprisoned that they'd stopped coming to the meetings. He didn't blame them, just felt sorry that they couldn't join in and worship God any more.

A warm glow came over him as he recalled the sight of the angel in the tunnel. Illusion or not, it had been quite overwhelming, and he wondered what it would be like to meet a real angel.

Chapter 9

Planet Trehf, Year 2099
(Population :30 million)

Scanning data. There are exactly twenty thousand people alive on the Planet Tirleen (untrue data, records are falsified). Birth and deaths are controlled by their leader, Zut. When a wizend (that is a person over eighty-five years) is due to die on their two hundred and fiftieth birthday, Zut will create new life using either a male or a female's main gene. The mother or father must be fifty years old, because they are not considered mature enough to mitose the new creation until then. The growth of the baby is then timed so that it is born at the exact time as the wizend dies, thus keeping their records straight and the population always exactly twenty thousand.

The creative stage lasts for nine days, during which time the baby is grown in the Mitosis Room and scanned daily to check its growth and acceleration rate. It is then introduced to the Transfer Room where they insert wires into the fourth lobe of the cerebrum to enable the lead at cerebrumadrome (learning center) to be plugged straight into it and feed it with information.

From birth to twenty-five, their brains are programmed at the cerebrumadrome for sixty wixons (one hour) every day (900 wixons in a day) to receive the knowledge and information Zut wishes them to know and, unknown to them, subconsciously controls them to follow his orders with subliminal messages.

At twenty-five they all join the Planet Force and either become guards, controllers, programmers, Searchers, or manuals.

At seventy-five they can register and become partners with the person they live with. Zut does not allow it before then as they change partners so often. If they are still with the same partner at seventy-five years of age they are allowed to sign a register and call themselves "partners until evaporation."

At exactly two hundred and fifty years of age they go to the Evaporation Room, where they die and their remains are evaporated into the air.

The temperature on the planet is always controlled at 70 degrees Fahrenheit and it rains for exactly sixty wixons (one hour) every seventh day to keep the water domes and streams full and sustain their plant and vegetable life.

All their meat is from animals cloned at the animal cloning market and their fruit and vegetables are genetically grown to ensure a constant supply. They consume large quantities of alcohol called galiquon, which is 78 proof. This is even fed to the babies at night to help them sleep.

They are taught by the Spirit Master that God does not exist and those few people who do believe (Faith Believers) have to hold secret meetings in tunnels. If they are caught they are imprisoned in life tubes (these are sealed tubes containing amniotic fluid and connected to a program that will keep them alive until their two hundred and fiftieth birthday, when they go to the Evaporation Room and die).

"That is disgusting." Fiona switched the screen off in disgust and looked at her father, Doug, who had tears in his eyes. "Are you all right, Dad?" She hoped she hadn't upset him by looking at this old data she'd found in his files.

"Yes, I'm fine. It just brought back painful memories reading it again," he said, rubbing the top of his head.

"Oh, poor Dad. I'm so sorry. It's just that I'm curious as to where we all came from."

Fiona stroked her father's head, being careful to avoid the large scar at the top. They all had one of these. Apparently it was where their brains were opened on the day of their birth and wires inserted for them to receive this knowledge that the awful man Zut wanted them to know.

Fiona knew nothing about her place of birth. Her father was one of the few lucky ones who'd managed to escape through a porthole they'd found near the animal cloning market one day when they were getting their weekly meat allowance.

On the few occasions her parents spoke about their old life, she'd gathered more information about where she was born and what life was like. She knew that her parents, Doug and Cedra, were one of the people called Faith Believers since they believed in God. When they saw their friends imprisoned in those life tubes they knew they had to find a way off the planet.

Her father was convinced that other planets existed and from stealing some data from Zut's headquarters, where he worked as a programmer changing all the data written by Zut, he had learnt all about the existence of portholes and what to look for. He had seen a shimmer and felt an electric energy near the animal cloning market and felt sure there was a porthole there. So, along with his friend Rone, also a Faith Believer, they worked out how to open it and planned their escape.

Rone and his wife, Hilary, had no children. The only child they'd had was born dead twelve years ago when something had happened in the birthing process. Cedra had said it was all very sad as up until then no one ever died before their two hundred and fiftieth birthday, but then lots of babies died, about one hundred in all. Zut was very clever and programmed the minds of nearly all the parents who'd lost their babies so that they had no memory of ever giving birth to them. Apparently, though, he wasn't as clever as he thought he was, because for some reason he was unable to erase the memories of fifty-two of them.

Hilary and Rone were two of those. They were absolutely distraught at losing their child, and when they heard from Doug that

Zut had been trying to program their memory to forget their daughter ever existed, they were horrified. Thankfully, those that did remember warned the ones due to create next what had happened, and when these people demanded answers, Zut found a fault in the acceleration process that killed the babies.

Working in the Program Unit, Doug was able to find out how much Zut controlled the planet, including the fact that he falsified the records so that even though all those babies had died, the population still showed as 20,000.

After their daughter died, Hilary and Rone attended more and more Faith meetings and it was when they were at a meeting with Doug, Cedra, Fiona and Jaycen that they were all caught by the Planet Force guards. Tears streamed down her mother's face on the few occasions she spoke of this, which was not very often as it was so painful for her to remember it. She said that they had kicked and punched the guards and fought like mad to escape, especially when one of them snatched Jaycen, who was then only two years old. Her father had hit him with such force that he knocked him out and they were able to rescue Jaycen and then ran to the back of the tunnel, praying that the guards would be distracted as they attempted to arrest the other Faith Believers.

Doug had discovered a boulder that, if forced, went into another hidden tunnel. He had found this out when he was looking for a hidden escape route to get to the porthole. The Planet Force must have been too busy arresting the other Faith Believers, because they never followed them down the tunnel and they were all able to reach the porthole.

Fiona was then only three years old and together with her brother Jaycen, had made such a noise screaming from fear that the adults were terrified they would be heard in the tunnel. It was a relief when they reached the porthole, but also some fear. They had no idea where it would take them to. It could be somewhere worse than Tirleen. Her father and Rone had checked it was safe to leave the tunnel and they'd all run toward the porthole and disappeared through it.

They found themselves in a field surrounded by cows, where it was pouring with rain. This apparently continued for four days and, as she now knew, this was quite normal here on Trehf where the weather wasn't programmed and could be quite unpredictable.

The noise she and Jaycen were making alerted the owner of the farm they'd landed on. They were in the middle of a field on land owned by Timi. He was stunned when he found them and despite the fact that they looked different to him with the wires coming out of the top of their heads, he had taken them to his home.

Here his wife, Gana, had fed them all and then put the children to sleep with their two children, Rex, who was one, and Pam, who was four.

Once her parents had gotten over their fear and realized that Timi and Gana were friendly, they had asked where they were. They were stunned to find they had gone back in time to the year 2099 and obviously were on another planet that Zut didn't know existed. *Or did he,* wondered Doug? They had all been programmed to believe that Tirleen was the only planet, yet he still sent Searchers out looking for other planets. He obviously knew they existed and knew about portholes, but either they hadn't found any other planets yet, or perhaps he had and destroyed them. Still, the adults felt they were well away from Zut now and safe on this planet called Trehf.

Timi told them that here they were used to "aliens," as he called them, popping in and landing on his field. They either found the porthole to come visiting their planet, or had lost their way on their travels and popped through by mistake. Whatever the reason they were all greeted and treated fairly by the Governors, unless of course they came intending to harm the Trehflons and try to take over their planet. Then Timi raised the alarm.

His home was disc wired straight to the Governors' headquarters. He and his wife, along with all the other Trehflons, always wore a watch that was programmed with an alert button. If this was pressed, it showed up on the alien alert panel that was constantly monitored in the Jet Quarters. If it started *bleeping* they could see immediately where the trouble was and send the nearest laser jet to destroy the aliens.

Timi had only found unfriendly aliens twice since he'd lived on the farm. The first time he had persuaded them that he would show them where his leader lived if they didn't harm him, and before he'd got very far the Laser Force had located them and put a protective barrier around Timi before lasering all the aliens.

The second time was much more frightening and he only just managed to get himself, Gana and the children into their Jetler and fly off before the aliens were able to stun them all. Apparently these were very strange aliens who had several fingers coming out of their bright orange bodies that fired some sort of electrical stun ray. Timi had been hit by one as he was fleeing and he said it hurt like hell, but he'd managed to get up and run and grab the rest of his family and at the same time alert the Jet Quarters. Luckily, because of the funny shape of these aliens, they were very slow at running. While Timi and his family were flying to safety, the aliens were being lasered by the laser jet crew.

He liked living here on the farm, though, so put up with the odd "visitor" popping in. Timi and his wife were one of the few families privileged to live and work on farms. Trehf was quite a big planet and over 30 million people lived on it. Most of them lived in large cities, but some of the planet had been kept open with green fields and the land divided up into farms. There was a waiting list to live on these farms, because although the quarters in the cities were luxurious and well run by robots for everyone, some people wanted to get back to the old ways and work hard and breathe fresh air instead of living in cities that were completely sealed and air controlled.

It was all very nice in the cities, but outdoor vacations were all the rage and people were going to special farmootels and helping the farmers out on their farms. Three days was normally enough for most of them when they realized what hard work it was, as well as dirty and cold, and the fact that it rained a lot. The few that enjoyed it put their names on the outdoor living list and waited for one of the present occupants to leave or die.

Timi had informed the Governors of their arrival and the next day they were all collected and taken to the main Governor's unit to register and check that they were peaceful enough to stay. Doug had told Governor Brent of what life was like on Planet Tirleen and why they had escaped. The Governor could see they were all very scared of returning to Tirleen and obviously not a threat to their planet, so had let them all stay.

They were delighted when they saw their living quarters. It was luxurious and with a robot maid, so different to their sparse dromes on Tirleen. Zut did not allow many of them to have such comforts, only himself and a few of the higher ranking Tirleens were allowed to live in such luxury. Here this was normal. The planet was not so advanced as Tirleen, but what a different atmosphere. Everybody was relaxed and welcoming, nothing was banned, and they were free to do anything they chose to.

They had been taken to the city care unit and medics had examined their heads to see what they could do about the wires in their brains. They had been horrified to hear that this was done on the day of their birth and were very surprised that the babies had survived such an ordeal. It was then that Doug and Rone wondered how many other deaths Zut had hidden and erased from people's memories. It was quite easy for him to create new life.

The medics were very interested in how life was created on Tirleen, which was why Fiona had been able to look up the data she had been reading. Doug and Rone had written all they could about Planet Tirleen, along with how life was created. As Doug had worked in the Program Unit, he was able to remember some of the programs for such things as creating life and evaporating people. This information was passed on to all the scientists on Trehf, who had used some of it and stored other pieces, such as creating life, away for future use. They preferred their old way here. Much more enjoyable.

Hilary had been very upset when she found out that on this planet she was actually not only considered too old to give birth but that women here could start creating life as young as twelve years old. It was then that she found out she was actually neither male, nor female.

They were all very shocked to find that although their bodies looked male or female, they had vital parts missing that actually decided what sex they were. When they saw what real men and women looked like they were very angry and realized how they had been duped by Zut. He told them if they were male or female when they were born, and now they realized what he'd done. They could see that their bodies were quite similar, just their faces were altered to look masculine or feminine.

The medics had called them asexual beings and when they were then shown discs of how life was created on this planet they realized what they'd been missing! Obviously Zut wasn't as intelligent as he thought he was. If he knew what he was missing, he would definitely have programmed the creation files differently!

The wires had been removed from Fiona and Jaycen's brains without any harm, but Doug, Cedra, Hilary and Rone still had a few wires remaining as they were too deeply imbedded to remove, which was why Doug's skull was tender and sometimes painful.

Hilary had died two years after arriving on Trehf. She'd been on a Jetler that crashed and the bang to her head had caused one of the wires to poke into an artery and she'd bled to death before they could save her. Surgery was not as sophisticated here and unlike Tirleen, where they were able to repair any damage to your body with lasers and programs; here people died from their injuries and even some illnesses.

It was quite a shock to Rone. He'd expected her to live to two hundred and fifty years of age, the same as on Tirleen. After her death he was so shocked he kept saying that perhaps life on Tirleen was better than here. If they had stayed there Hilary would still be alive. He'd forgotten how they weren't allowed to worship God and how the Planet Force guards nearly caught them. Hilary would be in a living tube until she died. That would be much worse than the two happy years she'd had here.

They'd been delighted when they found out they could openly worship God here, or any other faith they wanted to worship, of which there were many. There was no need to go to secret meetings.

Units had been specially built for people to go and worship how they chose and no one was penalized for whatever faith they chose to worship.

Rone got more and more depressed. Now that they were allowed to have and to show their emotions he'd realized how fond he'd become of his wife, Hilary. When they'd found out that you could marry here as young as fifteen years old, the two couples had chosen to be married in the House of God unit as soon as they could.

Doug tried to tell him that at least he'd married Hilary. He wouldn't have been allowed to on Tirleen until she was seventy-five years old. "Yes, but she'd still be alive there," he kept repeating.

Although she was only five years old at the time, Fiona could still remember her father coming in from a visit to Rone's unit and being very distressed. She could hear him saying, "He's gone and he's left a note saying he's going to the porthole and back to Tirleen." Both of her parents had sobbed and sobbed and kept on about living tubes. She hadn't a clue what these were then, but now she'd found out.

"Oh, Dad, will Uncle Rone be in one of those awful living tubes?"

Doug nodded, unable to speak. He was too upset to say anything. He'd tried to forget about Rone and what his fate would probably be. At the time he had just prayed that Rone hadn't shown Zut where the porthole was because he was terrified that Zut would send his Searchers here and that their knowledge would be so much more advanced that they would take over the planet and Zut would rule here, too.

He had informed the Governors and they'd put extra laser jets on alert, ready to fight and protect them at the first sight of any Tirleens, but so far none had come through the porthole, so they'd continued to live peacefully and happily here.

Doug put the image of Rone in a living tube out of his mind and told everyone to get ready to go out. He was taking them to the Jetlerscope to see the latest 3D screening. They all loved hovering in the air watching the film as it was projected onto a giant 3D screen in the sky. Except, of course, when it was a horror film and it felt like the monsters were coming out of the sky and after you!

Chapter 10

Planet Tirleen
God Speaks

"Mum, why won't Sirleen the great Spirit Master help us?" wept Anjoy as Viola hugged and stroked her hair to try and comfort her.

Anjoy was now experiencing fear, something else that was new to them. She didn't like it here, but she did love the feeling her mother was giving her when she touched her. She'd wanted to feel this touch from her for a long time and it gave her a lovely warm glow. It was almost as good as when God hugged them.

Viola was still fuming with their leader. How dare he hit their child. She also couldn't understand what all the fuss was. Why wouldn't he let then take their children home to meet the rest of their families? Odraine would be flabbergasted and shocked, but then overjoyed. Just as she was when she realized that Anjoy was alive.

Viola wondered how she could tell Anjoy that on this planet no one believed that God existed; he was just a fairy tale, and those few that did believe were severely punished. Edril, her wizend, had been right all along. God did exist and here was his proof. Why didn't Zut believe now? Here was a miracle right in front of his eyes, yet not only was he still denying God existed, but trying to convince everyone else that their children were programs, and as well as that—evil! These children were pure love. Couldn't he see that? Or perhaps he could and that was what was scaring him. Zut hated emotion of any kind. Perhaps he just didn't know how to deal with it.

They were joined by Sone, who was hugging her son, Broocen, and had a huge grin on her face.

"Viola, isn't this wonderful? God has sent us our children back. The Faith Believers were right all the time, weren't they?"

"Yes, and I hope Zut releases all those he's imprisoned in the living tubes now that he realizes they were right. It's cruel anyhow. Even when we thought that God didn't exist I always felt the Faith Believers weren't harming anyone by their beliefs."

"Nor me. Why won't they let us take our children home? I want to show the rest of the family our new son."

"Zut still believes that God does not exist. I think he is scared of him. He is trying to convince everyone else that our children are evil and programs as well as not alive, which of course we know they are."

Viola kissed Anjoy again. She loved the feel of her soft skin. It was so wonderful to be able to actually touch her and she couldn't hug and kiss her enough. The other parents and their children gathered around Viola and Anjoy. They'd been told by their child that Anjoy was going to lead them and tell them all what to do and where to get help from.

"Viola, why can't we go home with our children? Why are the Guardians ignoring us? They are just looking straight ahead as if we don't exist," asked Orliji's mother, Divinia. She had her arm wrapped tightly around her son's waist, terrified that one of the Guardians would take him away from her.

"They think they are just programs and evil and will harm them," Viola said, getting angrier with every wixon they were kept there.

Orliji looked at Anjoy. He was very scared. God had said they were going to bring great joy to this planet, but so far Anjoy had been attacked twice by the leader of the planet. She looked very scared, too, and she was going to lead them and tell them what to do. He wanted to go back to God. He didn't like it here even if his mother was lovely. The rest of the people were scary and it terrified him. Why couldn't they all go home to heaven? He sat on the floor and bawled. The tears running down his face frightened him even more. Now something else was happening to them. His face was leaking!

As he thought about this he brightened up. Perhaps he was dying and was on his way back to God. He sat and waited and the tears stopped. Why hadn't he disappeared, and why had his face stopped leaking? Perhaps it was because his mother was hugging him and he felt lovely and warm. He wanted to push her away because perhaps she was stopping this leaking and preventing him from going back, but then the warmth he was experiencing from her was as lovely as God gave them.

Anjoy looked at Orliji in despair. She was supposed to know what to do. God had said Sirleen would help them, but when she'd approached him he'd not only looked scared, but pushed her away. She wondered if God knew that Sirleen thought he didn't exist. Having heard her mother talking to the other parents, she realized they were all alone and that there was no one to help them.

How could she make this man Sirleen believe in God and get him to help them? It was going to be a harder task than they all thought. *Did God know that?* she thought. It was then that she remembered one of the last words he'd said to her before they all left heaven. "If you need help, pray to me. I will always hear you."

That was it. They must all pray to God. The more of them that prayed, the louder it would be and God would definitely hear and help them.

"Everybody kneel. We must all pray to God for his help," she said, getting on her knees and putting her hands together to pray.

"That's it, everyone," said Viola to all the parents. "We must ask God for his help and we must thank him for sending us back our children. Yes, we must definitely thank him."

They all sank to their knees and, following Anjoy, put their hands the same way to pray. Viola was right. God had sent them their children back and now they must show him how grateful they were.

As the parents and children knelt with their hands together, Bence averted his eyes and stared at them in horror. The other guardians did the same.

"What are they doing now?" one of them whispered to him.

"I don't know," Bence said.

Now he was terrified. Dare he move and call for help from the Planet Force guards? He was scared that if he moved just one muscle these "things" would turn and stare at him and overpower him before he got help.

"Hello, God. It's me, Anjoy," she said aloud.

Oh no, thought Bence. The terror he was feeling rapidly spreading to the other guardians as they realized these "things" were talking to this man, God. Perhaps they were programmed to get messages to this person who'd programmed them and he called himself God. He may be more powerful than Zut. What should he do? Ought he let Zut know what was happening? He had obviously been as scared of these "things" as they were. Why else would he place the Planet Force guards outside the Hologram Shrine to stop them from leaving and attacking anyone?

"God, we need your help please. The Spirit Master who you said would help us…" Anjoy struggled to think what to say. How could she tell their lovely God that Sirleen did not believe in him?

"Tell God that the Spirit Master is scared, that's why he won't help. Oh, and ask God how we can escape from here!" Viola said, tugging on Anjoy's arm to help her out.

She could see how embarrassed Anjoy was, trying to explain to the gracious man who'd sent their children back as gifts, that people on this planet did not believe he existed.

"He is frightened of us, God."

Anjoy nearly added, "and so are we," but decided if the Guardians heard how scared they were as well, they would let that nasty, horrible man who they called their leader know and he might cause more of that pain on them. She shuddered at the thought of it and wished God would beam them all back to heaven, with their parents, of course. Now they'd been touched, hugged and kissed by their mothers or fathers, whoever had been chosen to create them, they loved them as much as God and didn't want to leave them.

"Please help us go home, God. They won't let us leave."

Viola stroked Anjoy's hair and smiled at her. "Can I talk to God now? Will he hear me?" she said, not knowing if he could only hear the children or not, having never spoken to him before.

"Yes, just talk aloud to him. He hears everyone."

Anjoy was glad that her mother was trying to help as well. She felt a bit safer now. She wasn't sure she wanted to lead them any more. It wasn't going to be as easy as she first thought. When God said he was sending his little angels back as gifts to this planet, she thought everyone would be so overjoyed at their gifts that they would say sorry for all their bad ways and thank God for his gifts.

"God, it's me, Viola. Anjoy's mother. Thank you so very much for sending me my beautiful daughter back. She is lovely and I'm so very grateful and I'm sure the rest of her family will be as well."

As Viola sat down, the other parents took their cue from her and one by one spoke aloud thanking God for his gift of their child. Bence was now in utter despair. The parents were now talking to this God. Zut was right, these "things" had overpowered them and they'd become Faith Believers. It must be one of the Faith Believers who'd tampered with the Hologram Shrine program. Who, though, and how would Zut find out who it was? The Faith Believers were very clever and kept their secret hidden well. It could be anyone on the planet, even one of his Guardians. He looked around at the Guardians to see if anyone was smiling or giving any clues away to show they were pleased with these "things." All the Guardians, however, were trembling and sweating with fear now that the parents had also started to talk to God.

"Anjoy," said a deep voice.

Anjoy looked up and all around. That sounded like God's voice, but she couldn't see him anywhere in the room.

"Anjoy tell your mother you must use the teleport, and then be very careful. I will help where I can," the voice continued.

Anjoy looked around for God, but she couldn't see him anywhere. She knew she'd heard his voice. So where was he? The other children and their parents were all looking at her expectantly, waiting to be told what to do next. From their faces, none of them had heard God, only her.

"Ask your mother where the teleport is, Anjoy," insisted God's voice.

Anjoy suddenly realized she could hear God talking in her head. Now she remembered all she'd been taught. The older and higher angels had taught her that people living on different planes to them and on many planets could converse with them by opening and using their chakras. This enabled them to get to a level where they could hear the angels messages when they asked them for their help.

She could obviously talk to God whenever she wanted and hear his reply. She felt slightly relieved. At least she could still speak to God, so even though he wasn't with them he could help her in this great task.

Viola was watching her daughter. She seemed to be miles away and concentrating hard. It was such a great task for so small a child to perform. This God must exist, though, or how else would their children still be alive? It was then that a small doubt seeped into her mind. Were they alive? Perhaps Zut was right and someone had programmed them to live. That would be cruel, very cruel, if they had.

Edril was convinced there was a God. That was why she and others risked their lives to attend the secret Faith meetings. Surely they wouldn't do that if they didn't have any proof that God existed? Edril had spoken of angels and miracles and God creating the whole universe. There was a hidden tape with it all on. She hadn't seen it, but their leader, Zincon, and others had.

For once she wished Edril was there with them. She could do with her support. She was starting to lose the joy she first experienced when she realized Anjoy was alive and was now getting very scared. She wondered why God had told Anjoy to ask Sirleen for his help. Surely he knew his job was to tell everyone that God didn't exist? The small seed planted in her brain started to grow and make her doubt if her daughter was real or not.

"Mum," whispered Anjoy.

Viola jumped as Anjoy spoke. She had been miles away then as she wondered what to do and what really was happening. As she looked into Anjoy's eyes and saw how bright and sparkly they were, she realized that of course Anjoy was real. Nobody could create anything with eyes that looked right into you and filled you with so much love.

"Yes, Anjoy. Has God told you what we must do?" she whispered back, hoping that Bence and the other guardians couldn't hear them.

"Where's the teleport?" whispered Anjoy.

The teleport! thought Viola Of course, the teleport, that was how they could escape. She was just going to tell Anjoy where it was, when that little seed of doubt in her mind grew a little bit more. The teleport went straight to Zut's headquarters. The Hologram Shrine was the only unit where there was no teleport to go straight to it from their dromes, nor could it be reached by teleport from anywhere else on the planet. They had to use the flier and be teleported outside the shrine and the guardians would let them in. When they left, the guardians would alert the flier controller and when the flier appeared the controllers would teleport them onto the flier.

Zut, however, could teleport into any building he wished, so there was a teleport inside the shrine, but it led straight to his headquarters. Why was this God telling them to use the teleport? They would get caught straight away if they went to Zut's headquarters.

Viola hesitated, not sure whether to tell Anjoy or not, but then she looked into her eyes again and she was lost. Her motherly love took over and told her brain not to be so silly. God had sent her this gift and she must not doubt that he existed. That would be very rude of her.

"It's in the corner, but it leads to Zut's headquarters and that would be very dangerous for all of us to be found there. The guardians are keeping an eye on us too, so if we move they'll inform Zut straight away and he'll be ready for us."

Anjoy looked around the room. She could see where the teleport was, but her mother was right, the guardians would stop them and if it led to that horrible man Zut's headquarters he would hurt them all as soon as they arrived.

"God, why did you tell me to use the teleport? It goes straight to that nasty Zut's headquarters. He'll cause us more pain and that hurts, you know." Anjoy spoke to God in her mind so that the Guardians wouldn't hear her.

Anjoy hoped God would come up with another solution and waited quietly for him to speak.

"Anjoy, you all have to be very brave. The only way out of there is to use the teleport and then be very careful. If you can get to your dromes Zut will leave you alone for a while. He will be too scared to harm you."

Anjoy wasn't too pleased with God's reply. It was all very well telling them to be very brave. He was up there and safe, whereas they were down here and surrounded by people who could cause more of this pain thing.

"We have to use the teleport and try to get to our dromes. Zut will be too scared to harm us if we escape from here," Anjoy whispered to her mother, noticing how scared her mother looked at the thought of using this teleport straight into Zut's headquarters.

"How do we get to the teleport without the guardians harming us?" Viola wondered if this God realized how difficult it would be for them to even attempt to use the teleport.

"God, can you help us to get to the teleport, *please*," Anjoy added very loudly as she spoke to God in her mind again.

"Tell everyone to be ready to move," God replied.

Anjoy whispered this message to her mother, who then passed it on to Sone and it carried on around the other parents and children. They all sat quietly and waited for God's help.

Bence's ears had pricked up when the whispering started. He struggled to hear what they were saying. They were obviously planning something, but what? Suddenly a bright light appeared all around the children and their parents. Bence and the other guardians gasped in shock and fear. They couldn't see them anymore. This light was so bright that it hurt their eyes and they couldn't look behind it to see the "things" and their parents. They didn't know what it was, but there appeared to be a hologram in it of something white hovering around with feathers. What was it?

The parents stared at the angels. They were scared. What were these bright things? They were smiling at them, so appeared to be friendly, and were forming a circle around them as if they were helping them.

"Archangel Gabriel! Thank you!" screamed Anjoy in delight.

All the children ran and tried to hug Archangel Gabriel.

"We will stop them seeing you. Move quickly to the teleport, but be very careful when you get there," Archangel Gabriel replied.

The angels opened the circle so that the parents and children could get to the teleport unseen. They all stood in it and Viola nervously set the controls to teleport. Were they going to survive the next bit, or end up in living tubes with the Faith Believers? Bence would tell Zut that they'd spoken to God and in his eyes they would all be Faith Believers then. But were they? That little seed in her mind sprouted a bit more.

Chapter 11

Zut's Quarters

Viola was surprised. They were in Zut's sleeping quarters. She was expecting them all to be teleported into his working quarter, but instead they were here. She whispered for them all to be quiet. They'd gotten this far, much to her surprise. Now they had to get out and into their own dromes. How were they going to do it? Should they risk getting to the main entrance of Zut's headquarters, catching a flier and then teleporting into their own dromes? Or should they find another teleport, one that they could use to go directly into their own dromes? If they went for the latter idea then they would all have to take it in turns or end up in one drome all together.

She wondered if Anjoy knew what to do next, but she was gazing in awe at Zut's luxurious bedroom. It was indeed very luxurious. That was the first thing that had hit Viola when they found themselves here. Very luxurious indeed. Their dromes were very sparse and the seating quite uncomfortable, which was why so many of them spent most of their free time at the Galiquer, because that was also luxuriously furnished. A bit like this bedroom, in fact.

She knew Zut was their leader and had expected him to live in grander quarters than the rest of them, but was it fair that it should be this grand whilst theirs were so sparse?

Anjoy thought heaven was beautiful, but this bedroom was

almost heaven in itself. She walked up to the giant bed and touched the covering. It was so soft and silky. She sat down to see how soft it was. Mmm, it was heaven, just like sleeping on a fluffy cloud.

This was just the lead the other children needed. They had been dying to touch these beautiful things. Now that Anjoy was on the bed, they dashed around the room, picking things up, prodding them, and then to Viola's horror as she and the other parents tried to stop them touching things, the boys started jumping on the bed to see how springy it was. The girls joined them straight away so the boys picked pillows up to stop them and started hitting them to knock them off the bed.

"Stop! Stop!" Viola tried to whisper, but the children were having so much fun they didn't hear her. What was she going to do? The noise they were making was bound to attract the Planet Force guards. She looked at Anjoy, pleading with her to make them stop.

Anjoy stood on the bed and tried to stop Orliji, but as he thumped her with a pillow it burst open and feathers flew everywhere. Anjoy sat on the bed and giggled and giggled. This was fun. It was just like heaven with all the angels' feathers floating around. She looked up to her mother and to her horror saw tears running down her face and all the other parents' faces. She realized they were terrified of something, and when she stopped giggling she could see why. The children were making a lot of noise. God had told them to be careful at Zut's headquarters, and yet here they were alerting everyone to the fact that they were there.

"Quiet!" she risked screaming at them.

The other children were so surprised to hear Anjoy shout that they stopped what they were doing and shut up immediately. No one ever shouted in heaven. What was wrong with Anjoy? They were only having fun.

"We'll be found out if you carry on making this noise. We have to get to our parents' dromes and meet the rest of our families. Don't you want to do that?"

The children looked downcast. This was a boring place. Now they weren't so sure if being sent back was as exciting as it sounded.

So far Anjoy had been hurt and they'd been held prisoners, and even now they had to be careful they weren't caught.

Viola and the other parents surveyed the mess in the room. Zut's bedroom was a total disaster. Bedding, cushions, and clothes were strewn about and, worst of all, covered in feathers. They didn't have time to do anything about it now; they had to get out of here as quickly and as quietly as possible.

She hadn't a clue what to do, though. If they managed to get out and onto a flier, they would attract a lot of attention, but if they looked for a teleport in a corridor or somewhere they would all have to wait whilst they took it in turns to be teleported. That could take time and Viola was frightened the guards would find them as they waited.

"What do we do now?" Sone asked her.

Viola looked at Anjoy. She was starting to get cross with this God. Why wasn't he helping them? That was, of course, if he did exist and this really was her daughter. She hoped they hadn't all walked into an enormous trap.

Anjoy concentrated and spoke to God, asking him for his help. He told her they were to use the teleport again and go straight into their own dromes. He would make sure nobody tried to attack them whilst they used it.

"God has said that we must find the teleport and go straight to our dromes. He will stop them from attacking us."

Viola wasn't too sure how this God would stop the guards from attacking them, but then he had sent this bright light down into the Hologram Shrine so that they could escape. Perhaps he was real.

She cautiously touched the panel on the wall and it opened into a corridor. She peered out and to her relief saw that they were alone. The parents and children quietly walked along the corridor until Viola found the teleport. Sone and Broocen went first. The one wixon it took to teleport them to their drome and back seemed like an eternity. By the time there was only Viola, Anjoy, Jenna and her mother, Grathe, left, Viola was covered in sweat. She had never been so scared in all her life. All the time they were waiting she had been praying to this God. "Please help us, God," she said over and over again.

"Mum!" whispered Anjoy.

Viola stopped praying and looked at her.

"God is very pleased with you for praying to him."

Viola suddenly realised what she'd unconsciously been doing. Praying. For the first time in her life she had prayed. Edril had spoken to her about prayers many time, always when they were alone, of course. Even Edril's wizend partner, Epsone, didn't believe in this God, so she was very careful when she spoke of him or attended secret meetings. If Epsone ever found out he wouldn't hesitate to report her to Zut.

Viola breathed a sigh of relief when Jenna and Grathe left and the teleport came back for them. They got in and she entered the code for their drome.

Chapter 12
Anjoy Meets Her Family

Odraine and Ashtez were on the hard floor. It was such a relief to finally be allowed to sit down after standing for so long, especially with all the galiquons inside them. They were both trying to concentrate and answer Captain Braze's questions whilst their heads were thumping and spinning all the time. They still didn't know why they were under drome arrest. Captain Braze had suddenly disappeared and when Odraine finally plucked up the courage to ask one of the Planet Force guards where he'd gone to, he was told to the Hologram Shrine.

As soon as their captain disappeared, the other guards relaxed a bit. This was when Odraine and Ashtez were finally allowed to sit down. What was the point of making them stand? They weren't too sure what they were guarding them for, just following Zut's orders.

"Wow!" exclaimed Ashtez.

Viola and Anjoy suddenly teleported in front of her and Odraine. She'd been nodding off a bit from the galiquons and had the shock of her life as she opened her eyes and could see her mother's legs in front of her, along with another pair. She looked up to see her mother smiling and with her arm around another child. A female child.

"Who is that?" she asked, a little worried now. She didn't recognize her at all. Where had her mother found her? Is this what all the fuss was about and, if so, where had she come from?

Viola looked at Odraine's shocked face. "You know who it is, don't you?"

Odraine slowly got up and touched Anjoy. He wondered if he was asleep and dreaming after all the galiquons he'd consumed. *Of course not,* he thought. They were programmed not to dream, so this person next to Viola who looked like the hologram of their daughter Anjoy must be real.

"Anjoy?" he whispered.

"Hello, Dad. Yes, God has sent all the children back as gifts to this planet. I'm alive."

"Wow! Wow! Shut her up! Take this thing away," said Ashtez, panicking. She jumped up and tried to push Anjoy out of the door.

"Leave your sister alone," screamed Viola, trying to protect Anjoy.

The Planet Force guards stared at Viola and Anjoy. They had been wondering who this child was and what they should do, but when she had spoken the name of God, they had gasped in shock and fear.

"Faith Believers, you are under arrest," said Cole, who had been left in charge.

"Mum, how could you bring a Faith Believer into our home? You know you don't believe in this God and hate all Faith Believers," Ashtez said desperately, then turned her attention to her father. "Don't we, Dad?" Her eyes were pleading with him to stop staring at this "thing" and stroking its hair.

She grabbed Odraine by the arms and tried to pull him away and bring him back to his senses. What did he think he was doing? Did he want them all to be arrested and put in living tubes just because their mother had been brainwashed by the Faith Believers? Who or what this "thing" was she didn't know and didn't care. She just wanted her out of their drome.

"Zut knows about our daughter. You can ask him if you like. He has let us come home and he wouldn't do that if he wanted her arrested, would he?" Viola said, hoping her bluff had worked. If the

Planet Force guards would just leave then it would give them time to escape again before they realized she had lied.

Cole blinked his eye twice to connect with headquarters. Viola panicked as she watched him do this. She had forgotten all the guards were programmed so that their wires were connected to receive and send messages telepathically to headquarters.

Cole was allowed to speak to Zut personally, so told him of the new development. Zut was in his sleeping quarters as he listened to Cole. He was surveying the mess and wondering who, or what, had done it. He felt sure that whoever had made that program had done this. A sort of calling card to let him know how powerful he was and that he could get in wherever he wanted unseen by anyone.

Zut felt terrified and powerless for the first time in his life. He had sent Sirleen away to see if he could find out where any Faith Believers were and see if they could make them say who their leader was. So far none of those they'd caught would admit to who their leader was. They all kept saying that God was their leader and he suffered for them, so now they would do the same for him. He would help them. *Stupid fools,* he had thought. Fancy allowing themselves to believe in a fairy tale and to suffer so horribly for it as well.

He listened as Cole said one of these "things" was in Viola and Odraine's drome and talking about God sending her back as his gift. *Damn that person who changed my program,* he thought. He had to find out who it was and fast. He was starting to look weak and a fool amongst the people, but what could he do? Somehow these "things" had left the Hologram Shrine with their parents and perhaps they were all in their dromes now. He had left strict instructions that no one was to interrupt him and Sirleen whilst they decided what to do about this situation, so perhaps the Planet Force guards had been trying to contact him.

Dare he risk arresting them? He thought for a while, but felt it was too risky as he remembered their eyes. That was obviously how they'd escaped. They'd hypnotized the Guardians and then the Planet Force guards who were outside the shrine. He told Cole to leave them there and to come back to headquarters with all the other Planet Force guards. He was dealing with the matter, because these "things" weren't real, he assured Cole, just programs.

Cole was absolutely astonished. He stared at Anjoy. Not real? This was a really good program. Not only did she look like she was alive and breathing, but she could speak. No wonder their leader sounded rattled. This person who had made this program may well be more powerful than Zut.

Anjoy turned to look at Cole as she realized he was staring at her and wondered what he was going to do to her. Cole panicked and looked away and ordered the rest of the Planet Force guards to leave immediately and not to look into the "thing's" eyes as it would hypnotize them. They all left as quickly as they could.

So that was it, thought Ashtez. That's how their mother had been brainwashed into believing in this God. This "thing" had hypnotized her. Now she could see what all the fuss was about. Somebody had tampered with the Hologram Shrine program and instead of the holograms disappearing, these "things" had remained in their places. They'd obviously hypnotized all the parents into believing they were really their children and sent from God. Well, that wouldn't be too hard to do in her mother's case. She was very gullible and easily fooled.

Ashtez had to admit that whoever had made the program had done a very good job. She was very impressed and could see why Zut would be angry. Zut was very, very angry, in fact. Damn her mother for being so gullible. She'd just remembered that if Zut was angry and thought her mother was listening to this "thing," hypnotized or not, then he wouldn't give her a job as a Searcher.

She glared at her parents, who were both gazing down at Anjoy. Now her father had been trapped as well. She wasn't going to be that stupid, as long as she didn't look into her eyes, she'd be all right.

Anjoy sensed her sister was scared of her. She felt sad. She'd so looked forward to meeting her brother and sister, but Ashtez seemed very angry with her for some reason. She was just going to speak to her, but jumped in fright when Hurlen teleported into the room. Hurlen looked at his parents and Anjoy in astonishment.

"Who is that?" he said, pointing at Anjoy.

Viola smiled, took his hand and brought him closer to Anjoy. "This is your sister."

Hurlen looked at Anjoy then at Ashtez. "No, it isn't. That's my sister," he said, pointing to Ashtez, then added, "and she can be a pain sometimes, so I certainly don't want another, thank you."

Ashtez smiled gratefully at her brother. At least he was on her side. Hurlen totally ignored his parents' protests that Anjoy was his sister too and started to unpack his lenses.

"Hey, sis, the Planet Force guards are everywhere. They've surrounded some of the dromes and the Hologram Shrine. Something big must be up. Do you know what it is?"

"That thing," Ashtez said in disgust as she pointed toward Anjoy. As Hurlen looked at Anjoy, Ashtez screamed out to him. "Don't look at her eyes whatever you do, she'll hypnotize you." Hurlen quickly shut his eyes.

Viola was now undecided what to do next. Her husband knew who Anjoy was and was obviously overjoyed to see her. He hadn't stopped kissing and hugging her since they'd come home. Ashtez and Hurlen, on the other hand, were a problem. She remembered that they had never visited the Hologram Shrine, so of course had no idea what Anjoy looked like. It was going to be hard to convince them that she was their sister and alive now, especially after Ashtez heard the guard saying that rubbish about her hypnotizing them. What utter rubbish. If only they looked into her eyes, they would realize how much love she sent out.

"Hurlen, this is your sister who died at birth. God has sent her and the other children back as gifts to the planet to help people realize he exists."

Hurlen gasped in horror. His mother had mentioned the word God and was talking as though he existed. No wonder Ashtez was worried. They could all be in serious trouble if the Planet Force heard her. He'd thought he would come home to find his mother and father really proud and overjoyed at Ashtez being the new Wiron Leader. Instead, his mother had some person with her who she called her daughter, and worst of all was talking about God like a Faith Believer.

"Ashtez, perhaps we should go to the Galiquer and let Mum and Dad spend some time with, with…" He couldn't bring himself to say her name.

"Yes, good idea," she said, grabbing Hurlen and pressing the teleport. They both disappeared before Viola could say anything.

Odraine looked at Viola. "Don't worry, it's a shock, that's all. They'll come around and love her as we do."

Viola smile gratefully at him. Thank goodness he believed her at least.

Chapter 13
Round One to the Spirit Master

Hurlen and Ashtez lined the straws of galiquon up in front of themselves. They had no intention of going home whilst that "thing" was there and their mother was talking like a Faith Believer. They intended to stay with Dad's wizends if she didn't go away. They'd be safe from the Planet Force there, because if Viola kept talking about this God, she and their father would be arrested.

There was a lot of noise coming from the adult section and Hurlen was trying to decide whether it was screams of laughter or screams of fear. Ashtez looked at him. She could hear it, too. A group of children were peering into the adult section, curious to see what all the noise was about. Ashtez and Hurlen got up and joined them. To their horror they could see their parents and they had that "thing" with them.

Anjoy and the rest of the children were in a group with all of their parents. Hurlen could hear cries of, "Don't look at their eyes," and "Why haven't they arrested them yet?" Whatever were his parents thinking of, bringing her here? Ashtez was right, she had hypnotized them. Why else would they do such a stupid thing?

All the children who were watching ran backward as they saw the "thing" approaching their section. "Run, run," they were screaming, "don't look at their eyes." Ashtez and Hurlen ran and sat down, hoping against hope that their parents wouldn't join them, but worse was to come. Anjoy and the angel children stood in the center of the children's section and Anjoy started to speak.

"God is very angry with you all. Children should not be drinking, and you certainly shouldn't be getting drunk ever."

As the children laughed and laughed at her, Hurlen and Ashtez curled up and tried to hide. They were so embarrassed. They hoped no one realized she was with their parents. Ashtez frantically tried to signal to her father to take the "thing" and her mother away, but Odraine stood beaming with pride at his daughter.

Edril has been right all along, Odraine thought. God did exist and they needn't be afraid of people knowing they were Faith Believers now, as Anjoy had said this God was going to help them all. First they had to try and change all the bad ways on the planet, such as Zut controlling everyone and taking all the tirns people paid for food and drinks and furnishing his section lavishly and not allowing anyone else to have such luxuries. Viola had told him about Zut's quarters and he was as shocked as she had been. God had told Anjoy that Zut was programming their minds to follow his orders without questioning it. No wonder they'd allowed themselves to live in such sparse quarters whilst Zut lived so well.

Sirleen sat in the adult section, listening to Anjoy's speech. He was worried. How was he supposed to help Ashtez now? All that effort into becoming the new Wiron Leader and her hopes of being a Searcher were now gone. Zut would strip her of her title when he arrested all the family. *Unless,* he thought. Yes, that was it. Unless he could persuade Ashtez to live with her father's wizends. She would probably still lose her title and her hopes of being a Searcher, but at least she'd be alive. Her mind was too brilliant to be locked away in a living tube.

He sat pondering on the problem of these children/things and how to find out who had programmed them. Zut had told him about all the feathers in the bedroom. This person was very clever leaving a message to make it look like angels' feathers, but then was he leaving them a clue that he was a Faith Believer and he was going to make everybody believe in this God when he took over the planet? That would be the end of his work as the Spirit Master. What would this person do to him? Would he find some way to get rid of him?

As he sipped his straw of galiquon he watched Jayfer getting more and more drunk and more and more angry. He wondered why. Jayfer was Sone's partner and the parent of one of these "things," so why wasn't he with the other parents? Why wasn't he happy? They all seemed overjoyed at "God's gifts" as they kept calling them. Perhaps this was the answer to his problem. He fetched four straws of galiquon and placed them in front of Jayfer.

"You're not happy that this God has sent Broocen home to you, then?"

"Broocen! Who is he?"

"I thought he was your son. That's what Sone calls him. She seems overjoyed at God's gifts."

Jayfer looked at Sirleen through his blurry eyes. What was he up to? He was talking as if he believed this God did exist, but he was the Spirit Master. He'd been telling everyone that God didn't exist. So who was right here? This "thing" Sone said was their son who'd died twelve years ago and apparently had been sent back by God, or the Spirit Master who had always told them that God was just a fairy tale? He drank another straw of galiquon.

"Ah, but is he real? According to you, God is a fairy tale. So how can a fairy tale create this thing Sone calls our son?"

Sirleen leant closer to Jayfer. "I'll let you into a secret, Jayfer, shall I?"

Jayfer nodded, anxious to hear what Sirleen was about to say.

"They are not real, just programs. Somebody got into the Hologram Shrine and altered the program so that instead of disappearing, these "things" remained. He was very clever because they look so real and they can speak."

"I knew they couldn't be real because there isn't anyone called God. He's just a fairy tale."

"You have to be very careful. They are hypnotizing people to believe this God exists. Zut thinks one of the Faith Believers has done it."

Sirleen waited whilst Jayfer drank two more straws of galiquon before making his next move.

"Would you like to help Zut get rid of these things? He'd be very pleased and would reward you really well. You could move to very luxurious quarters in return for helping our leader."

Jayfer was all ears, he'd do anything to live in better quarters, even if it meant upsetting Sone by getting rid of this "thing" she called Broocen. He must make her realize it was only a program before she got to attached too it.

Jayfer could barely walk because he'd drunk so much, but he managed to reach Sone and Broocen without falling over. He persuaded her to go home at once by tricking her into believing that he wanted to spend some time with Broocen, their new son. Sone was overjoyed. At last Jayfer realized their son was real and a gift from God. She called their other child, six-year-old Denna, to join them. Denna was drunk, like her father, and Broocen looked at her with disapproval. He was so horrified at the sight of all the children getting drunk. God would be so angry with them.

They all teleported home, as Jayfer and Denna could barely walk to the flier station. Once there, Denna promptly fell asleep on the floor. Broocen was asked to watch her whilst Jayfer spoke to Sone alone. Broocen sat next to Denna and stared at her. *God was right,* he thought. This was a bad, bad planet. All those children drinking and getting drunk, and his sister, in fact his very small sister, was one of them. It was terrible.

He surveyed their quarters. Cold, sparse and very uncomfortable. As he did so, he remembered how luxurious Zut's and the Galiquer were. No wonder people all went to the Galiquer if all the quarters were like this. God had said all the tirns spent on the galiquons went to Zut, which was obviously how he furnished his quarter so well. It was more welcoming at the Galiquer than their dromes and it encouraged them to drink and give him more money.

"I'm so glad you accept Broocen is our son now, Jayfer," said Sone, smiling. She had been so delighted when he'd suggested coming home to spend time as a family and getting to know Broocen.

Jayfer could barely stand, let alone talk, but there could be a lot of tirns involved here and better living quarters, so he had to be very careful how he phrased what he was going to say to her. The difficulty was his head was spinning and tact was needed here, as Sone had obviously become very attached to this program. Tact was something he'd never practiced before. In fact, he was a bit of a bully and more often threatened people. He worked in the Planet Force unit programming the many changes in the laws that Zut made and the Planet Force guards ensured were carried out. He used this knowledge to bribe people and warn them when the Planet Force guards were checking up if they'd carried these laws out. All the money was spent on the galiquons he consumed every evening. Zut was well aware of this, but it was to his advantage to turn a blind eye, as all the tirns Jayfer received in bribes came back to him via the Galiquer.

"Sone, you must realize this 'thing' is just a program created by one of the Faith Believers to hypnotize people into believing in this God. When everybody believes then he is going to take over the planet as leader."

"It's not true. I know it's not true. Broocen is real." She wept.

She desperately wanted her son to be real. She'd been overjoyed when he remained instead of disappearing and at first thought Zut had planned it so that they could feel them before they disappeared. Whatever the reason, it was lovely to touch her son. He was so grown-up now.

When Broocen had told her that he had been sent back from God as a gift, she'd been horrified. God was a word they never used unless to laugh at. God didn't exist, so what was her son on about? She wasn't sure what to think or do, but then they hadn't disappeared and the guardians had become more and more nervous and finally summoned Zut and the Spirit Master. Neither of them looked very happy when they saw the children, so obviously Zut hadn't planned it.

Zut told them that somebody had tampered with the program and created these "things" as he called them, and they weren't real. From then on it got more and more frightening. The Planet Force guards were summoned and the parents and children were kept locked up, but had managed to escape with Viola and her daughter's help.

Jayfer watched Sone's face as she took this information in. Now to use the ways he knew best—lying.

"I've been told by someone who knows the person who was responsible for tampering with the program."

"Oh no!" she wept. Why couldn't it have been true? She so desperately wanted to believe he was real.

"So we are all in danger whilst that 'thing' is here. Zut will think we are all Faith Believers." He waited a while and then added very dramatically, "And you know what happens to them."

Sone's eyes grew wide with fear. Jayfer was right. What a fool she'd been. She'd put the whole family in danger bringing this "thing" home. She listened as Jayfer told her what Sirleen had suggested.

Chapter 14

Planet Trehf
Gabriel Asks for Help

Fiona woke with a start as she jumped back into her body. She had a thumping headache from speed traveling. It must have been a long way to Tirleen. She wondered if it was wise to astral travel there. She hoped it wasn't the future, as it was an awful place, but then it was only thirty years ahead of their planet, so it couldn't possible be the future. Could it? Her father thought that because they came through a porthole that it was an entirely different plane and so Tirleen would never be their future again. Besides, people had been programmed for centuries not to believe in God on Tirleen. Whereas on Trehf you were allowed to worship any religion and nobody had scars where wires had been put in the fourth lobe of their cerebrum to program them.

Should she tell her father what she'd seen? What could he do if she did, though? She knew he never wanted to go back there. It was far too dangerous. Unlike poor Rone. It was a bit of a shock seeing him in one of those living tubes, staring at her. She knew it was her astral body traveling and not her real one, but she felt sure he could see her. His eyes seemed to be pleading with her for help. The shock of seeing him had nearly sent her astral body back to her physical one.

Then she saw this child with the most beautiful eyes staring at her.

The child had been trying to hold hands and send comfort to another child, who also had these beautiful and deeply comforting eyes when they looked at you. The child was crying as she looked at the boy in one of those awful living tubes.

Somehow Fiona found that she could communicate with the girl telepathically. She said her name was Anjoy and God had sent her and other children back from Heaven as a miracle to help this planet believe in him, but it was harder than they thought. Broocen, the boy in the living tube, was put in there as an example to show the people that Zut did not believe these lies. The "angel children" were only programs and anybody who believed these children were really sent from God would join him in the living tube.

Anjoy had suddenly panicked as if she'd seen something and had quickly ran away. Fiona followed her and found herself in a tunnel full of adults and children. They all looked scared and desperate, but before she could ask Anjoy what was happening, she'd jumped back into her physical body. Was this awful headache from speed traveling and jumping back into her body so fast, or from the pain she felt for those people?

She got up and joined her family for breakfast. Her mother noticed how tired she looked and wondered whether to take her for a check up at the City Care Unit.

"Are you feeling all right, Fiona?" she asked as she felt Fiona's brow for any signs of a temperature.

"I slept badly. Nightmares, that's all."

Doug stopped eating and looked at her. She did look very pale and tired.

"I knew I should not have let you see those files on the Planet Tirleen. I hope there's no way the small amount of programming you received there is still hidden deep in your brain cells and reading about Tirleen has activated something that will cause problems."

"Dad, stop worrying. The nightmare was all about monsters. Probably from that 3D film we saw last night."

Fiona kissed them both and hurriedly left for the Learning Center before they could ask any further questions.

"Doug, you look tired too," Cedra said, suddenly noticing the dark patches under his eyes.

"I slept badly as well. Archangel Gabriel was back asking me to help the Faith Believers on Tirleen."

"Was it a dream because those files have opened up memories for you?"

"No, he's appeared many times even when I'm awake. But I can't go back there, Cedra. I'm too scared of what will happen."

Cedra got up and made him a calming herbal drink. She didn't want him to go back either. It was a dangerous place. He would be caught and put straight in a living tube and they may make him say where the porthole was and come and get the rest of them. Or even worse—she quickly made herself a herbal drink as this thought came into her head—even worse, they could take over planet Trehf. Her hands shook with fear as she took a sip.

Doug watched Cedra as they drank. He could see how worried she was. He knew he could never tell her that he'd meditated and astral traveled there and seen how bad it was now. Even worse than when they'd lived there. God had sent Tirleen a miracle and they were ignoring it, and more and more people who did now believe in God were either in living tubes, or hiding and fearing for their lives.

He decided he would go and discuss it with Governor Brent. He was a very wise man and if Zut ever found the porthole, then Trehf would be in danger, too, so the governor needed to know so that they could be ready to stop an attack. He may also know of a way that Doug could help his friends back on Planet Tirleen.

Chapter 15

Planet Tirleen
Zincon Is Caught

Sone looked at Broocen staring at her through the living tube. Had she done the right thing? Jayfer said they were only programs made by one of the Faith Believers to try and take over the planet. But were they? His eyes seemed to be pleading with her and it looked as if tears were in his eyes. She didn't know if they were real or part of this program.

Jayfer had taken Broocen, she couldn't get herself to call him "it" or "thing" even if he was a program, to Zut's headquarters where he'd been prodded and scanned to see where the wires or program were hidden. To their dismay, however, nothing had been found. Zut was even angrier. Where was the program to control it? If he could find just one program he may be able to decipher it and break all the other things' programs.

Zut had put Broocen in a living tube in the hope that those people who still believed he was real would get scared and perhaps give the other things up for him to examine. At least it showed the people that he was still in charge and would be very ruthless with anyone who still said that God existed.

With a heavy heart, Sone walked away. Broocen's eyes had disturbed her. It was almost as if he was suffering and wanted her to help free him. She shrugged the thought out of her mind and headed toward their drome.

As she touched the soft silky furnishings she realized that Jayfer was right. That "thing" was just a program. She loved living in this luxurious drome that Zut had given them in return for handing the "thing" over to him. They were very loyal subjects, he told them, and if the other parents did the same they could also live in dromes like theirs.

She had tried talking to the other parents, telling them they had been duped by a very clever Faith Believer who'd altered the hologram program and made these things. They might look real, but they weren't.

None of the others would listen to her. God had sent them their children back as a gift. How could she let her son suffer so much? They were all praying for him in his pain and hoped that God would find a way to release him. Jayfer was furious that the other parents wouldn't listen to them. Keeping this luxurious drome depended on them persuading the other parents that their things were just programs, too.

The longer they kept saying that God existed and these things were his gifts, the angrier Zut got. He desperately wanted to put all the children and their families in living tubes to show he was in charge of Tirleen, but was just a little scared of arresting any of the others. This Faith Believer was so clever. He'd got into his quarters and left his calling card and he'd also found a way for them to escape from the Hologram Shrine, so how easy would it be to capture all of them without this person causing him any harm? These children and the problem of what to do with them were in his thoughts all the time. It was very difficult to run the planet efficiently whilst all he could do was think about them and who was responsible for them.

In the Evaporation Room, Zincon was wondering about the so called "angel children," too. He was trying to decide whether they really were gifts from God, or if somebody was playing a joke on Zut and trying to take over the planet. Had that angel who appeared before them been real, and were they to help these children? Or had this programmer found out who the Faith Believers were, and in particular who their leader was, and was trying to trick them into betraying themselves?

This programmer could be trying to catch all of the Faith Believers together to show the rest of the planet that he was not only more powerful than Zut, but far more intelligent. Zut had only managed to find a few Faith Believers so far. This was either a very devious person using God as a trap to take over the planet, or perhaps on the other hand they really were gifts from God. Was this all down to just a question of faith? he wondered. Perhaps God was testing him, too.

His belief note that week had been all about the word "belief," and how strong theirs was. Even if these children were just a program, was their belief strong enough to accept they were God's gifts to show that it could be possible? He carried on thinking about the question of whether they were real or not as he tucked that week's belief note under the body of the next person to be evaporated. Silently he blessed him and wished him luck on his journey, then went to press the evaporator.

"Stop!" screamed Furnise.

Zincon jumped. Trepidation ran through his body as he wondered if he'd been seen putting the note under the body. He turned and saw Furnise rushing toward him, so he quickly put his hand up to press the evaporator, but before he could reach it Furnise had pushed his hand away and thrown him to the floor.

"What were you putting under the body? I saw you do something."

Zincon watched in horror as Furnise moved toward the body and slid his hand underneath and found the belief note. Furnise was smiling as he read the contents.

"What's this, then? Looks like something a Faith Believer would have. Don't tell me you're a Faith Believer, Zincon?"

Furnise could not believe his luck. He'd been watching Zincon for a while and had felt sure he was up to something but didn't know what. This, however, was wonderful. He'd caught a Faith Believer! He'd actually caught a Faith Believer. He studied the note more closely and his smile turned to a huge grin as he realized what he'd found. The proof was here in his hands for their leader to see. How pleased he would be with him.

Zincon watched him read the contents and slowly got up from the floor, hoping Furnise wouldn't notice him. He knew he had to escape, and quickly, and was intending to try and get to one of the tunnels and hide there, then plan what to do next.

"You're the leader of these Faith Believers, aren't you?"

Furnise was ecstatic. He'd not only found a Faith Believer, but their leader. Zut would be so pleased with him. This must be worth a lot of tirns, as well as moving to luxurious quarters. If Jayfer and Sone had gotten wonderful quarters for giving up their thing so that Zut could warn the other parents, then what would the leader of the Faith Believers be worth?

He panicked as he realized Zincon knew he'd been found out and was trying to escape. He had to stop him somehow. He couldn't afford to lose him. It was no good just giving this note to Zut without Zincon. Anybody could have written it. In fact, Zut might even think that he had written it and was one of those awful Faith Believers. What was he going to do? Zincon was far younger and stronger than he was. How was he going to stop him from leaving?

Zincon realized Furnise was scared of him. Only the two of them were in the Evaporation Room that day as thankfully not many people were due to be evaporated. All he had to do was push him over and run to the teleport and he'd be free. The note by itself was not proof. He could say that Furnise had written it. He prayed to God to help him and ran toward Furnise and grabbed him by the shoulders and threw him backward. As Furnise fell, he dropped the note, so Zincon quickly picked it up, then ran toward the teleport and screamed as he bumped into Jayfer, who had just teleported into the room.

"Stop him, Jayfer," yelled Furnise, who couldn't believe how his luck was going today. Here was help in the form of a very powerful man. "He's a Faith Believer, don't let him escape."

Jayfer couldn't believe his luck either and without questioning Furnise, quickly thumped Zincon in the face with such force that he knocked him unconscious. He, too, was thinking that it must be his lucky day. He'd only come to the Evaporation Room to ask them to a galiquon gathering to show off his luxurious quarters, and here he was helping to catch a Faith Believer. This would improve matters with Zut. He was getting a bit impatient with him because he hadn't persuaded any of the other parents to give their children up to him. He'd even been hinting about taking their quarters away from them, which was why he was having the galiquon gathering. He wanted to show everyone how generous Zut could be if they helped him persuade the other parents to give their things up. Capturing another Faith Believer would be a bonus and Zut would surely let them keep their quarters now.

"Good work, Jayfer. Zut will be very pleased with us. Zincon is not only a Faith Believer, but I think I have the proof that will show he is also their leader."

Furnise was so pleased it had been Jayfer who'd teleported into the room. He had no qualms about hitting anyone. He had definitely been placed in the wrong position when he was chosen to work in the Planet Force unit as a programmer. Jayfer was a bully and loved to use his fists. He was surprised that Zut hadn't noticed this and made him a guard in the Planet Force instead.

Jayfer looked at Zincon sprawled on the floor. All he could think of was all the tirns it would bring him and perhaps even better quarters than they lived in now. If Zincon was the leader of the Faith Believers, then dare he risk bargaining with Zut?

"You drag him to the teleport and I'll follow with the note," said Furnise, quickly joining them and taking the note away from Zincon. There was no way he was going to let Jayfer take all the credit for capturing Zincon. He'd been the one to realize who he was in the first place, and besides, he had the proof—the note—in his hand. That must be worth a lot more than just knocking Zincon out. He hoped Zut would be pleased enough to move him into one of these luxurious quarters, too.

Chapter 16
Torture and Death

Sirleen was with Zut as they checked the hologram program again, hoping to find some clues as to who could have tampered with it, when Captain Braze's face appeared on a screen in front of them.

"Yes?" snapped Zut. "What do you want? Can't you see we are busy? I distinctly told you we weren't to be disturbed."

"Apologies, leader, but I have news that will interest you."

"Well, get on with it. What news?"

"Jayfer and Furnise have not only captured a Faith Believer, but we think he may well be their leader, as Furnise has found a note that he'd written."

Zut looked at Sirleen, his expression turning from anger to one of exhilaration. At last they'd found the programmer of these things. Now they could destroy them all and he'd be back in full control once again.

"Take him to the Wiring Room, Sirleen, and I will join you there," he said as he actually gave Captain Braze a smile.

"He is already there and wired up, waiting for you," said Captain Braze with a smile, partly from the fact that he'd received a smile from their leader, which was very rare indeed, but also from anticipation. This was one part of the job he loved best. Attaching somebody to the wiring unit and watching them scream in agony as it electrocuted their body was fun. Unfortunately, it didn't happen very often. The last person, that child thing, had been a great disappointment. They hadn't found any wires anywhere to use. They'd knocked it about a bit, and even though it had screamed out, it hadn't been so much fun. After all, it was only a program, it was probably programmed to yell out when hit. No fun in that at all, but this he was looking forward to. Their leader was ruthless. He would show no mercy toward Zincon and would keep going until he admitted to being the programmer of these things. He hoped Zincon didn't spoil things and give in to easily.

Zut and Sirleen quickly teleported to the Wiring Room. Sirleen was as pleased as Zut was that they'd finally found the person responsible for programming these things. Perhaps now these visions of those angels would finally go away. He was beginning to doubt all that he knew and programmed for everyone else about this fairytale God as the visions kept repeating themselves in front of him. He was fairly sure it was all the work of this programmer, but on the odd occasion he allowed his mind to wander and wonder if these things were real and that God did exist.

As the charge went through Zincon's body, his screams could be heard all around the planet. Zut had deliberately opened the intercom up to all the quarters and units and even stopped all the programming at cerebrumadrome and programmed this in so they could all hear how ruthless he would be with anybody hiding a Faith Believer or saying these things were God's gifts.

Captain Braze gleefully pressed the switch to put yet another charge through Zincon's smouldering body. He ecstatically watched Zincon yell and writhe in agony as the charge went through him, turning him blue then black, then smouldering as he burnt inside. Every time his body died he was brought back to life by putting his body through the laser program until his cells regenerated and he was reborn.

"Just tell me how you did it?" yelled Zut in frustration. Why wasn't this working? Zincon was being tortured and yet he still refused to say that he was the programmer and tell them how to get rid of these things.

"It wasn't me," sobbed Zincon. "Have mercy on me please, Zut."

"But you are a Faith Believer and also the leader of them, aren't you?" continued Zut. He was determined to find out how Zincon tampered with the hologram program and made these things.

"No, no, no, I'm not," yelled Zincon. "I'm not a Faith Believer. It's all a mistake."

Zincon suffered even more inside. Now he'd denied God existed and he was supposed to be the leader of the Faith Believers. God would be so angry with him, but he couldn't suffer this agony anymore. Why wasn't God helping him? He had prayed and prayed to him to stop this pain, but it hadn't happened, so perhaps there wasn't a God and he had been putting his life at risk all this time for nothing.

"You were seen putting the note under a body to be evaporated," persisted Zut, and at the same time indicating to Captain Braze to press the switch again.

"Nooooh!" screamed Zincon as he sizzled and fried, then died once again.

As Zincon's body was put into the laser program his soul floated upward and he found himself staring into God's face.

"Why have you denied me, Zincon? I am always with you and helping you."

"I'm sorry, God, but the pain was intolerable. I just couldn't cope with it anymore. Why didn't you stop them hurting me?"

"Perhaps your faith wasn't strong enough. All the time you were being questioned you were asking yourself whether it was worth believing in me and suffering the pain as you weren't sure whether I really existed or not."

"Oh, God, I'm so sorry. Please forgive me."

"I forgive you, Zincon, and I will help you."

Zincon winced as his body was rewired to the wiring unit. Had he imagined that conversation? God's face had been so kind and gentle. He hoped that he hadn't been hallucinating. A bright light appeared in front of his face as the charge went through his body again, and he felt his cheek being kissed by something soft and gentle. He realized that he felt no pain at all and gave a small smile of relief.

"Thank you, God," he shouted out.

Zut looked at Captain Braze in horror.

"You idiot. What have you done? You haven't wired him up properly. Why is he smiling and feeling no pain?"

Captain Braze hastily checked the wires and switches again. He couldn't find anything wrong. What was happening here? He'd seen the charge go through Zincon's body, yet he'd not only smiled, but he'd thanked this God person, too.

"So you are a Faith Believer then, aren't you?" yelled Zut as he stomped around the room in frustration. Why wasn't this working? He wanted these things destroyed, but Zincon was still trying to control him, even from here.

"Yes, I am a Faith Believer and the leader of the Faith Believers," said Zincon, this time with pride. "God has been very good and sent you many gifts to show he exists and yet you still deny him, Zut. Why?"

Zincon smiled as he watched more angels hovering around him and sending him peace and tranquillity as they took away all his pain entirely.

"Perhaps he's tampered with this program, too?" said Captain Braze, desperate not to get blamed for the wiring unit not working. Zut was in a very angry mood at the moment, so nobody was safe.

Zut looked at Zincon's smiling face. That was it! No wonder he'd smiled as the charge went through him.

"You have! You've altered this program as well as the hologram program, haven't you?" Zut said, realizing that Captain Braze was probably right. Had all those other screams that sounded as if Zincon was in agony been put on to make Zut think he was suffering, too?

"I haven't altered any programs. All the children are real and alive. They are gifts from God. Why do you still deny God exists

Zut? The proof is right here, those dead children are now alive."

Zut had never been so angry in all life. He pushed Captain Braze aside and pressed all the switches, pushing the charge as high as it would go. Zincon's body smouldered and sparked and then caught fire. Zut and Sirleen jumped out of the way as the guards put the flames out.

Sirleen watched as Zincon's body was put back into the laser program. He could swear that there was a light hovering above the body. What was it? He knew he hadn't had any galiquons yet, but he could see one of those angel's faces again as it hovered over Zincon.

He rubbed his eyes and watched in disbelief as he saw Zincon float away, smiling, with the angels holding him. Surely this wasn't possible? Zincon's body was here. How could Zincon make this happen? He must have programs hidden everywhere. Angels did not exist and there was only one Zincon, so where had this other one come from? He looked to see if Zut had noticed anything, but Zut was too busy checking the wiring unit to see if it had been tampered with.

"Well, hurry up, then. I want him back on this unit as soon as possible. He will tell me how he's done this program, you can be sure of that!" yelled Zut as loudly as possible so that the whole planet could see he was still in charge and would break this man, whatever it took.

Zut looked at the laser programmer's worried face and watched as he frantically pressed switches and changed controls and programs. Zut silently gestured to Captain Braze to switch all the intercom controls off and restart the cerebrumadrome program. Something was wrong and he didn't want the planet knowing about it.

He waited until Captain Braze had completed his task and walked over to Mander, who was still frantically pressing switches and looking puzzled.

"What's wrong? Why isn't he reborn?"

"I don't know, leader. Nothing is working. He's still dead," said Mander, desperately and frantically trying to work out what was wrong with the machine. The leader of the Faith Believers was in it and he'd killed him. Well, technically he hadn't killed him, but his job was to regenerate and make him alive again, and he'd failed. Zut would not be pleased with him.

"He can't be dead. Nobody dies until they are two hundred and fifty years of age," yelled Zut, who was now extremely angry that they'd finally found the programmer and he'd outwitted him yet again.

"I'm sorry, leader, but I can't do anything to bring him back to life," wept Mander fearfully.

As Zut frantically tried to reprogram the machine, Sirleen stared at the angel who was hovering above Zincon's dead body and smiling at him. Once again he started to wonder if Zut had been wrong all along and that God really did exist. *Whoa,* he thought to himself, and shook his head hard to get rid of such a thought. Whatever was he thinking? Of course God didn't exist. This was just a very clever trick that Zincon had programmed. Zut would soon regenerate him and bring his body back to life.

Chapter 17
Planet Trehf
Governor Brent Helps

Doug looked very tired as he sat in Governor Brent's quarters. The angel had not let him sleep at all that week. Every time he tried to close his eyes, a bright light would appear and Archangel Gabriel would be standing in front of him. He kept asking him to help rescue God's gifts. They were all hiding in tunnels, fearing for their lives, and only he could show them where the porthole was and help them to safety.

Doug knew Archangel Gabriel was telling the truth. He hadn't mediated and astral-traveled to planet Tirleen any more, but he had automatically astral-traveled there in his sleep. Probably when he was so worried about all his friends. In particular, Rone's tortured face staring at him out of a living tube was with him all the time and really distressing him. Why, oh why, had Rone gone back there? Surely he knew what his fate would be?

Governor Brent passed Doug another drink with a herbal tonic in it. He needed Doug to be alert to give him all the information he needed to rescue these people. He wouldn't normally risk sending any of the laser jet crew on such a mission. They were quite happy to welcome friendly aliens here, but he didn't intend going out looking for any that needed their help. This time, however, it was different.

Doug had explained when they first arrived here how nobody on Tirleen believed that God existed and those few that did were tortured if they were caught, which was why he and his friends had to escape that night and ended up on Trehf.

He'd since used astral traveling to go back there and see what had happened to his friend Rone, who gone back through the porthole. It was now even worse as God had sent Tirleen some gifts to prove that he existed. When the holograms of twenty-five children who had died twelve years ago had been switched off, they remained there instead of disappearing, but now they were alive. Despite this, the leader of the planet still refused to believe that God existed and those Faith Believers who hadn't been captured and put in some sort of horrific living tube were hiding in tunnels and starving.

Governor Brent had spoken to the leaders of all the faiths on their planet and they'd all agreed that such a gift was indeed a great miracle and if Archangel Gabriel was asking for their help to rescue these people, then they must do all they could to help.

"Can you remember where the porthole is that you came through to enter our planet?" Governor Brent asked, noticing that Doug looked more alert now. It was vital Doug remembered the exact spot they arrived on the planet. He didn't want them finding another porthole and ending up lost on some other planet and not be able to return to Trehf.

"I think so. We were right in the middle of the field and there was a large tree nearby. It should be easy to find."

From the little knowledge Doug had gained on portholes, he also knew the importance of finding the exact spot. He didn't want to end up a prisoner himself on another planet.

"I need to know more about Planet Tirleen and in particular this man called Zut. He sounds far more advanced in technical knowledge than we are, so we are going to have to try and work out how to outwit him," said Governor Brent, hoping he would understand everything he was told.

He had been horrified by the wires implanted in Doug and the others brains, but he also realized that the person who had created all the programs to make it possible must be a very clever person. When he realized what Zut was capable of, he had placed the laser jet crew on twenty-four hour alert in case Zut found the same porthole and invaded their planet. He wasn't sure the laser jets would be strong enough to kill someone with Zut's knowledge, but it was all he could do to protect their planet.

As time went on and there was no sign of anybody coming through the porthole, he relaxed and forgot all about Tirleen and being invaded. However, now he had to send some of his force on to the planet to fight and rescue people. It would need very brave men indeed and he wasn't sure if he could order any of the force to do it. He just hoped they had enough people brave enough to volunteer to go with Doug.

He could see that Doug wasn't too keen to go back himself, but it was a bit difficult to ignore a message from an angel. Especially such a persistent one as Archangel Gabriel.

Doug tried to remember all he could about Zut and how he ran, or rather controlled, the planet. It was difficult, as he'd spent the last twelve years erasing it from his memory whilst he learnt what it was like to live in peace and freedom. He shuddered as he recalled their sparse quarters, the food they had and how drunk he used to get. The only pleasure they had was sitting in the Galiquer and getting drunk on galiquon, the only drink available on the planet. Now he knew why. All the tirns went straight back to Zut to keep him in his luxurious lifestyle.

As he was remembering how Zut controlled them, something clicked in his mind. That was it! Zut used programs to control everyone. Surely on Trehf there must be somebody clever enough to know how to break or sabotage the programs?

"Zut controls everything through his programs. He has a brilliant mind and changes all the main data himself. Nobody is allowed to change anything. Once he has written, or rewritten, a program, it is then passed to the programmers to enter all the data on the relevant files," said Doug, hoping that this small bit of information would help the governor.

Governor Brent thought about this. They had many things controlled by computer programs, but not to the extent planet Tirleen did. He tried to think who would understand how Zut's brain worked and who could outwit it, or change any of his programs. The laser jet crew could fight and defend their planet, but they would not be any help in breaking programs.

"Is there any way you can get Angel Gabriel to come when you call him, or does he just appear?" Governor Brent asked.

Perhaps Angel Gabriel could give them a clue as to who would be the best person to send to deal with the programs. It was vital they sent the right people on this mission. It was going to be hard enough to find the exact porthole, let alone fight this leader and bring all the angel children and their parents back here to safety.

Doug though for a while. Angel Gabriel had always appeared either in his dreams or when he wasn't expecting him. He would just sort of turn up in front of him. He didn't know if he could just call him and get him to appear. His faith taught him that the angels were always with him all the time, looking after and protecting him, but he didn't normally just see any of them floating around or appearing in front of him. This was a totally new experience and if Angel Gabriel hadn't been asking him to do something he feared, then it could have been quite a pleasant one. He wished Angel Gabriel had chosen someone else to appear in front of. He had been trying very hard to forget everything there was about Tirleen, not having to remember it and go back there and face all the horrors it would involve.

"Can't any of the spiritual leaders tell us how to contact an angel when we need to? Surely one of them must know how you do it?" Doug said, thinking they stood more chance of rescuing everybody and coming back alive if the angels could give more information about what they were to do when they got there.

Governor Brent pressed a button on the wall and ten minutes later they were joined by Cordelius, leader of the White Light. He listened as Doug told him all about planet Tirleen and how Zut controlled everyone. Cornelius knew how to channel and talk to the angels and ask for their help, but he wondered if he could teach Doug how to do it. Yes, Angel Gabriel had appeared in front of Doug several times, but it was when he wasn't expecting it and so couldn't allow his mind to doubt what he was seeing or hearing. When you channeled to speak to angels, you had to be totally relaxed and listen to what they were telling you and most of all trust what they were telling you. Doug was so anxious he would start questioning and not hear what was being said to him.

"I will go back to my sanctuary and channel with the angels myself and see what advice they can give us. As soon as I have connected with them I will write it down and let you know their answers," said Cordelius, who was anxious to help as much as he could. One did not ignore messages from angels, and when God sent such a miracle as the gift of twenty-five children reborn from the dead, then you certainly didn't ignore him.

He wasn't sure if he was brave enough to go on this mission with Doug, even if the angels would be with him. He would go and talk with the angels and see what they advised and what they wanted him to do. If they wanted him to go, then he knew they would protect him somehow. He just hoped that wasn't what they were going to ask of him.

Doug left Governor Brent pondering over the question of who to send with him. He had done all he could so far to follow Angel Gabriel's orders. He had asked for help and it was coming. The trouble was only he knew how ruthless and cunning Zut was and the thought of returning to Tirleen, even if it was to save all God's miracles, was terrifying.

Doug returned home and looked through all his files on Tirleen again. It was a long time since he'd been there. Twelve years, in fact. There had probably been many changes. Zut liked progress and riches. He must have made many changes to his programs by now. He tried to remember what he'd seen in his dreams and astral travels. The living tubes were still there, although more of them. Everything seemed the same. He couldn't think of any changes.

He visualized himself flying around the planet and remembered that the Galiquer was bigger now. Yes, that was it, the Galiquer was bigger! That wouldn't help much, though. All the people did there was drink and enjoy themselves. He went back into his vision and found himself flying past the Galiquer, over the Celestdrome and Evaporation Room and over...he stopped. Something was coming back into his mind. There was a new drome. What was it, though? He remembered thinking how big it was, and bright. It was obviously another drome created by Zut to make him richer, so it must be something that would be used a lot. There was a lot of different lights and flashes coming from it and lots of weird noises.

"Come on," he kept saying aloud, "think, think, you can do it."

What did people do for pleasure on the planet apart from drinking? That was all he could think of. They drank, even the children. Although, of course, the children often had their lenses with them as they attempted to play their lens games, if they weren't too drunk and could see what they were doing.

Jubilantly he screamed out, "Got it!"

At last he'd remembered what the new building was. A Lens and Games drome. No wonder it was busy and also probably making Zut very rich. The children loved to use their lenses or play on the screens to try and beat the wires. Was that the answer to their problem? Zut would have built and programmed everything in that drome. Doug didn't know why, but he felt the answer was connected to that drome and it was staring him in the face, but he just couldn't see it yet.

Chapter 18
Channeling

The chimes from the music were ringing loud and clear in the White Light Sanctuary. Cordelius was trying to raise the energies in the room before he channeled and spoke to the angels. When he felt it was significantly high enough he opened his chakras,* made sure he was well grounded, then attuned and asked for his highest guide to come through and protect him on his journey to the angelic kingdom.

Now he could safely channel and talk to the angels. When he was sure the guides he had connected with had come from love and light, he started to ask them the questions that were needed by the governor for the rescue mission.

"Who will help us on our quest to save the children?" he asked first.

"The person you need lives on the planet, but first you will have to convince them that God exists."

Cordelius wrote the answers automatically, without questioning it. That would break the trust and he would not know if he had answered the question or the angels. Sometimes the answers didn't make sense until you read them back again and thought about them.

"How will they help us?"

"Their knowledge of wires and computers will match Zut's and they will be able to outwit him. Their help will come unexpectedly. You will think you have lost and will not survive and then help will come."

Cordelius asked the question he was dreading most, but knew he had to ask anyhow.

"What help can I give in this quest?"

"You must go and raise the energies of the other people on the mission as well as those in need on the planet. The energy on Tirleen is very low. Already the dark angels are starting to cover the planet and smother the light and lower the energy."

Cordelius thanked his guides and closed his chakras down, then made sure he was well grounded. He needed his mind clear to think about everything he had written. Now he knew his task was to accompany Doug and the laser jet crew. He struggled to stay in control and keep his energies high. Any negativity on his part would bounce off and affect the others and they would lose all confidence about rescuing the people.

He rewrote the angels' messages so that the governor could read them. He'd written their replies so fast that at the moment it was practically illegible. Luckily, though, he was able to decipher what he'd written. He was very worried about this person on the planet who would help them, but not until they thought they'd lost. He didn't like the sound of that. Why hadn't there been somebody on Trehf whose knowledge of computer programs matched Zut's? They would have been far more useful on this mission and could perhaps destroy some of the programs and make their mission easier. He sighed as he realized he was not trusting what the angels had decided would help. A lack of trust from him, the leader of the White Light, would definitely not do!

Governor Brent looked at the messages. He wasn't sure if they were of any help, but Cordelius had spoken to the angels and even though he himself was afraid of what lay ahead, he was prepared to go because the angels had asked him to do so.

He had managed to get eight volunteers from the laser jet crew, including their leader, Vonick, who had decided he could not let any of his men volunteer unless he went with them. With Doug and Cordelius that would make ten. Surely that would be enough? He hoped that they could just pop in through the porthole, find the people in the tunnels and bring them straight back through the porthole. Doug had said that he knew where the porthole was, so perhaps no fighting would be involved.

Chapter 19

Planet Trehf to Planet Placillon
Year 4010

The ten men stood in the middle of the field and waited and waited as Doug felt for the energy to try and find the open porthole. They were all anxious and sweating. None of them really wanted to go on this mission, but it was an order they couldn't refuse as it came from the highest authority there was—God.

Doug's hands pricked and tingled; the energy felt strong. He sweated even more, not from fear, but anxiety. He knew he had found a porthole, but was it the right one? It had to lead to Tirleen, because if it didn't he hadn't a clue where they would end up. It was in the exact spot, well from what he could remember when they arrived through it twelve years ago. His knowledge of portholes wasn't that fantastic, and he wasn't sure if they moved all the time or just stayed in the same place. He had to trust that this was the correct one. It was the only porthole he'd found on the field so far anyhow, so it must be the right one.

"This is it, the porthole. Here it is!" he yelled jubilantly to the others.

They all joined him, not knowing how scared he was of walking into the unknown. He had spoken so confidently that they felt sure it was safe to enter this porthole. The crew walked, or rather fell into the opening of the porthole. They landed on their feet and looked around at the strange planet.

"I was expecting Tirleen to be different to our planet, but this is much prettier than I was expecting," said Cordelius.

They looked at the blue rocks that were everywhere and the strange coloured ground. To their eyes it appeared purple, but then seemed to shimmer and change to pink, then yellow then grey. It was very odd. Doug had never mentioned any of this when he spoke of Tirleen, just how awful it was.

"It's quite pretty, almost a spiritual place. Perhaps this Zut man has been taken over and the angel children have managed to persuade the people that God exists. I think we are worrying over nothing. I can't tell you how relieved I am anyhow," said Cordelius, smiling for the first time since they'd left Governor Brent's office.

The others were staring at Doug, fear was in their eyes. Cordelius looked at Doug to see what was wrong. Doug's eyes were also wide open and full of fear. Cordelius started to tremble as he sensed all of their fear. Something must be wrong. But what? As Doug spoke, their fear increased.

"It's not Tirleen."

"Where is it then?" gasped Cordelius. He could barely speak since his throat had dried up with fear.

"I don't know. The porthole must have moved. I haven't a clue where we are."

Vonick decided to take control of the situation. At this rate they would let their fear control them and soon they would all be quivering wrecks and not able to help anybody.

"Cordelius, stop shaking. You've already said how pretty and spiritual it is. How can anything that looks this calm have people living here that we should fear? They are probably very friendly as we will see when we meet them."

They all listened to Vonick. He was right. What on earth were they worrying about? Just because it wasn't Tirleen didn't mean the people here were unfriendly.

They just had to find somebody to help them into another porthole. Only the correct one this time!

Vonick's advice was not just incorrect, it was very, very wrong. What he should have advised them to do was get out as quickly as possible. It was too late, though; now the rescuers needed rescuing.

They were surrounded by ten very strange beings. They looked almost human. Well, their faces did, but they had enormous fat abdomens and their umbilicus was ball shaped and about six inches wide as well as round. They didn't appear to be wearing clothes, just some sort of purple skin that covered all of them except the umbilicus area and that was white. Their arms looked as if they had been put on a rack and stretched, or perhaps it was because they had very short legs and small feet.

If the crew hadn't been so terrified, they may have found these beings quite comical as they stared at them, wondering what was going to happen next. They soon found out. Shooting out of these beings' umbilicus was some sort of string that started to wrap itself around each of the crew. Only as it got tighter and tighter did they realize it wasn't string but elastic. They found their arms and waist completely encased in it and then it stopped. Once the beings were satisfied they had their prisoners tightly encased they used their index finger, which looked like a razor, and cut it. The elastic that was left whirled back into their umbilicus.

Doug didn't know whether this was one of those times to speak and tell them they were friendly and meant them no harm, or whether to keep quiet. He chose to remain silent. He didn't want to be singled out as their leader and perhaps interrogated and even tortured.

"Move," said the tallest being. They didn't hesitate and followed the beings at once. They had only walked a short distance when the ground started to feel different. Instead of firm to walk on, they seemed to be sinking. Doug looked at the other men. Sweat was now pouring down all of their faces. The fear had been replaced by absolute terror. Were they all going to be suffocated in some sort of quicksand? they wondered.

The deeper they sank, the faster they moved, until they found their heads completely covered. To their relief and surprise they found they could breathe. They didn't know what was happening, but at least they could breathe and weren't dying a slow, agonizing death.

Suddenly they found themselves whirling around and feeling as if their skin was being tightened or shrinking. Doug was aware of a pair of silver eyes staring at him. He stared back, unable to move his head or any other part of his body. He wondered what they had done to him. Did he still have a body? he wondered. He couldn't feel any part of it and although he knew he had a head, he couldn't use his lips. Perhaps they had gone as well and all he was left with was his eyes?

"I will ask you some questions," said the face with the silver eyes, "and I want you to nod that you understand."

Doug's eyes stared back at the face. This was it, they had singled him out as the leader. He hoped that whatever they did to him wasn't painful. There would be no need to torture him, he was so terrified he would tell them whatever they wanted to know. That's if he still had a body left to torture, of course. He couldn't be sure of anything at this moment. The whirling had made him very dizzy and something painful had happened to their bodies, so perhaps he'd already been tortured?

"Will you tell the truth to my questions?" continued the face.

Doug rapidly nodded his head. Now he could feel he still had his head. Was that a good thing or not? he wondered.

"Good, that is wise. In that case I will remove the seal from your lips so that you can speak."

Doug felt a strange sensation as if a zip was unfastening on his lips, then to his joy he found he could move and open them. He licked them all around to feel them.

"Owwwwwwch!" Doug screamed, as he soon found out that he still had his feet as well. The skin on the toes seemed to be getting tighter and tighter and then they felt as if they were being cut off.

"That is just a taste of what will happen if you don't tell us the truth," said the face.

"I will tell you anything you want to know, but please, please don't hurt me again," Doug begged as he sobbed in agony. His toes had stopped being squeezed and were now throbbing so much he desperately wanted to have arms to hold them with.

The face was joined by ten other beings, including the tall one who'd led them here. He was obviously their leader as he told Doug his name was Bontril and asked what they were doing on the planet Placillon. There was only enough air for the people who lived there, so they could not allow them to live in case they brought more of their people onto the planet.

Doug hastily told him that they had no intention of living there, or bringing more people in. He told Bontril about trying to get to the planet Tirleen on a rescue mission, but the porthole must have moved because they'd found themselves here instead.

Bontril looked at his fellow beings. It was as if they were talking to each other telepathically, because their strange silver eyes seemed to be getting bigger and glowing. Then they shrank and stopped glowing. They had obviously been discussing what to do with them, and whether or not they were telling the truth.

"If you let us go, we'd go straight back to the porthole if you could show us where it was," Doug said, hoping this would please them.

"We do not know if we can trust you. We will think about it. We are quite safe from you at the moment, as you are all tightly encased in elastic wire. There is no way any of you can move."

"I…" Doug got no further, as his toes got tighter and tighter and the pain increased again.

"Silence!" snapped Bontril.

Doug nodded. From now on he wouldn't speak unless they requested him to. He'd learnt the painful way that you did as these beings told you to. He watched as they left the room. There were no doors or windows, just purple walls that looked like rocks or earth. He couldn't make out which. The beings just disappeared through it, whatever it was.

"Can anyone else speak?" he whispered, hoping they were safe for a while. You couldn't be sure with these strange beings. If they could glide through walls, then perhaps they could just appear in front of them.

There was a chorus of "yes" from the others. Doug was relieved to find he wasn't on his own. If only he could move as well as speak. As he was thinking this, the skin on his body seemed to stretch and he found himself wriggling his fingers. He still had his body! Cautiously he tried to turn his head and was delighted when it moved. Gradually he found that he could not only move every part of his body, but he could also sit up. He looked around and could see that the others had done the same and were all sat up looking very confused. Where was the elastic wire?

"Are you all right, Doug?" Cordelius asked. He'd been terrified they would torture him next.

Doug realized his toes has stopped throbbing and now felt as if cool water was pouring through them, taking all the pain away. Gently he felt his feet with his hands to check he still had five toes on each foot. They felt all right and yet it had seemed as if they'd been cut off. This was obviously mind torture. Whatever they'd done to him, he didn't want it happening again.

"Yes, I am, thanks. Whatever you do, don't argue or disagree with them! It was agony. I thought they'd cut my toes off."

He heard a sob and looked at Cordelius, who was openly weeping with fear.

"I thought the angels would protect us on this mission, but we seem to be on our own. Where are they?" he sobbed.

Doug moved off the couch he had been led on. His legs felt very strange, almost too tight, but at least he could still use them to move. He went up to Cordelius and took hold of both of his hands.

"Cordelius, what's happened to your trust?" If the angels have said that they will protect us, then they will. We are still alive aren't we?"

Cordelius nodded. Doug was right. At the first sign of trouble he'd lost his trust and faith in the angels. They would be there somewhere. He just had to believe they were with him.

"What's happening? What do you think they are doing?" asked Vonick

Despite the fact that he'd volunteered for this mission he was scared, too, but at least they'd experienced having to fight aliens who'd tried to take over their planet. These two had never had to face death or danger before. Although he'd heard that Doug had a terrible time on the planet Tirleen and only just escaped before he was killed, so he would have experienced fear, too. Perhaps it was good that they tortured Doug and not Cordelius. At least he had faced it better. Cordelius may have blubbered so much that the aliens may have decided to just kill them all. Cordelius's angels had obviously protected him and stopped him from being tortured.

Vonick hoped Cordelius wasn't going to be a handicap on this mission. He'd been in tighter spots than this before and at least they were still alive. For the moment anyhow! Somehow they had to try and escape and get back into the porthole. Even if they ended up somewhere else and not on planet Tirleen, surely it would be better than here!

Chapter 20

Planet Trehf
Through the White Light

Fiona was in bed praying. She hoped her father had gotten into Tirleen easily and was at this very moment showing the children and their families back to the porthole. Her eyes became heavy and she nodded off.

She found herself flying around the planet Tirleen. She was vaguely aware of being in the tunnels and seeing all the children huddled together with their parents and crying with their fear. She remembered trying to speak to the girl called Anjoy, but no words came from her mouth. She wanted to ask where her father and the rest of the rescue crew were. She couldn't see them anywhere.

A door banged and she sat up with a jolt. She was in her bed and the room seemed very bright. It was morning, so she'd been dreaming. She tried to remember what had happened, but it was all hazy. She had whizzed around the tunnels, she knew that much. Was it just a dream, or a nightmare because she was so worried about her father? Or had she astral-traveled in her sleep? You didn't normally whiz around places if it was just a dream. That only happened if you were traveling, especially speed traveling, if it was to somewhere a long distance away.

She rubbed her head where it throbbed so much. As she touched the crown, a vision of a silver cord came into her mind. The cord! That was it. She'd remembered the cord trailing behind her. So she *had* been astral-traveling. In that case, why hadn't she seen her father and the others? Something was wrong, she knew and felt that much. She wondered if Governor Brent would understand and be able to help.

Her mother and brother were still in bed as she let herself out and went to Governor Brent's unit. He was in the middle of eating his breakfast, so she apologized and then explained why her visit couldn't wait.

He invited her to join him with his breakfast, and she readily accepted. Eating may help her thumping headache so that she could explain herself better and not sound like an hysterical child to the governor.

Governor Brent listened as she told him what had happened in her sleep and how she was worried something had happened to her father and the crew. He explained gently to her that, firstly, if they were on Tirleen they may be hiding before they made their move and it could be several days or weeks before they returned, especially if they had difficulty in reaching the children and their families. Secondly, if they weren't on Tirleen, then they had no way of contacting them to see where they were or what was happening to them.

He could see he'd frightened her. Her eyes were wide open in horror and her shoulders had dropped in despair as she realized her father may be lost or even dead. Tears ran down her face as she wept and pleaded with Governor Brent to send another crew through the porthole to help them or see where they were.

If only it was that easy, he thought. Their knowledge of portholes was limited, but he did know that if it had moved just slightly, then Doug and the others could be on a different planet than the one they'd intended to visit, or even in a different time. They could have gone way back into time and then being held prisoners of very primitive people, or gone forward, which may be even worse, as knowledge there could be so advanced that they could possibly be doing horrific things to harm them. It was best she didn't know that.

"All we can do is wait, but if we do get a contact from them, then rest assured we will let you know straight away," he said, getting up and showing her out.

She went home with a very heavy heart, knowing she must help her father. But how, and who would help her do it? The walk through the greenery lifted her spirits a little. It may be created and covered by a glass dome, but listening to the birds singing and feeling the warmth on her face all helped her heavy heart a little.

Fiona blinked her eyes several times. An angel stood a short distance away. Was it Archangel Gabriel coming to help her? She ran toward the vision and her spirits lifted at the thought of getting help at last. She stopped dead in front of the angel as disappointment ran through her body. It was only a hologram. This was the entrance to the White Light Sanctuary. She'd forgotten this angel was always there.

It would take more than the hologram of an angel to help her father, she thought. Something like a real one and preferably Archangel Gabriel. At first she felt very angry with the hologram angel for flashing in front of her eyes. Then she realized that perhaps this was the angels' way of talking to her. Someone inside the sanctuary may be able to help her. Their leader, Cordelius, had gone on the mission, albeit reluctantly, but he had still gone to help. He had taken the angels with him to guide and protect them all. His followers would be inside here and if he'd taught them correctly, then surely there would be somebody who could help her?

She walked through the hologram, thinking how right they were. Her energy was higher and she felt far more positive. Here was the answer to her prayers. Somebody inside would show her what to do.

The sound of waves rolling in and out on the shore was relaxing and Fiona could almost visualize the scene and imagined herself on the beach, watching them. She'd never been to a beach or seen the sea, except on computer programs, but this was wonderful. Every muscle in her body loosened up and she felt at peace with everyone and everything.

She joined the people on the floor in a circle. They all had their eyes closed and seemed to be so relaxed that they were almost in a trance state. She didn't want to disturb anyone by asking questions, so she patiently sat and waited. She relaxed even more and all the tension in her body seemed to disappear.

A strange feeling started to go through her body. She was now so relaxed that she could hardly feel any part of herself and yet it seemed to be moving. She felt something inside herself going up and down and her legs seemed to be rising. She opened her eyes and looked at them. They were still on the floor. It was such a pleasant feeling that she closed her eyes and just let the feeling carry on.

She hovered above her body and looked at herself on the floor, cross-legged and with her eyes shut. It was all very strange and got even stranger when she saw bodies going into the people still on the floor. She watched them open their eyes and then turn to look at her body on the floor. Could they see her floating above them? She waved, but nobody waved back or looked up to her.

"She's definitely out of her body. I saw her floating there as I came back into mine," said Samuel, one of Cordelius's followers.

The rest of them agreed that they'd also seen her floating above her body. Fiona watched as Samuel knelt down by her body and gently stroked her arms.

"You must come back to your body now, little one," he whispered.

Fiona suddenly realized that she had actually astral projected through meditation. That meant she could just travel wherever she wanted to. She could go and find out where her father was. *How wonderful,* she thought. She was just telling her mind to find her father when she felt a bump and heard Samuel talking to her.

"It's OK, it's OK. It's always like that the first time. It gets easier. I can teach you if you'd like me to."

Slowly Fiona opened her eyes and looked at Samuel smiling at her.

"Bit of a surprise, wasn't it, finding yourself out of your body?" he said.

"I really did it! I was out of my body through meditation, wasn't

I?" she said, still feeling as if she could just float away if she wanted to.

She looked around at everyone. They were all smiling and nodding at her. Fiona told Samuel that she astral-traveled a lot in her sleep, but now desperately needed to astral travel through meditation, only so far she hadn't managed it. He listened as she told him of her dreams and how she felt her father and the others were lost or in danger.

"You were so worried about your father that until you came here you were too stressed to reach total relaxation and allow your astral body to project," Samuel said.

He explained that now she had managed it, the next time would be a lot easier, but she had to learn to travel slowly and safely. She couldn't just speed travel millions of miles away the first time, it would take up too much energy and stress her body. She had to learn to get used to traveling out of her body and just travel around the corners of the room the first time, then next time she could travel around their planet and after that it would be safe to speed travel and go wherever she wanted to.

Fiona felt disheartened. All her energy dropped and sadness took over her body. She thought that now she had managed to get out of her body through relaxation she could be off and find her father and the others. Samuel noticed and felt her sadness. Gently he explained that if she tried to travel too far too soon she would feel ill and be unable to travel for a while, so if she found her father she would be unable to travel back and get any more information if they needed help.

Fiona realized he was right. She had finally learned to get out of her body, so now she had to learn how to do it properly and how to control it. She listened and followed as Samuel showed her how to close her chakras down and then how to ground herself properly. He didn't want her going home with any of them open and feeling so spaced out that she didn't know where she was going or what she was doing!

The rest of Cordelius's followers quickly introduced themselves and congratulated her on her first travel. Zeb and Sooth were going to dowse Fiona's chakras to see if any needed healing before she ventured any further on her astral travels; they needed to be in perfect condition to ensure her energy was high enough to cope with the traveling. Angelico was going to accompany her each time she traveled until she was able to speed travel alone. Although Samuel explained to her that when she did go looking for Doug and the others, he and a few of Cordelius's followers would come along, too, so that they could all see what was happening and if they needed any help could all remember what they'd seen.

Today Fiona had gone far enough and couldn't attempt any more traveling until the next day, so very reluctantly she left the sanctuary and went home. She felt a bit flat now. The initial exhilaration of being able to project had gone and she was feeling impatient now. Having to wait a whole day before she could project again was boring. She could project now, so why couldn't she do it again straight away? Didn't Samuel realize she had to find her father and the others and quickly?

She was debating whether to try and project on her own and find her father, but then she remembered Samuel's warning. If she tried to project too far before she'd learned how to do it properly, then she may feel very ill and not be able to do it again for a while. If she ignored his warning and traveled today, as well as finding herself in the wrong place, she would also be unable to look until she felt better. Fiona realized that they were right and decided to use the time to find out as much as possible about Tirleen from all her father's data, so that she knew where places were and what happened on the planet.

Samuel discussed their visitor with Zeb, Sooth and Angelico. They had all felt that something had gone wrong with the mission. They could feel Cordelius's sorrow. Samuel had tried looking for Cordelius when he traveled, but for some reason had been unable to find him. He didn't understand it; normally he could ask to see someone and he would find himself with them, but today it hadn't happened.

They all agreed that Cordelius must still be alive because if he'd been killed then they would have seen his spirit when they asked to find him. Why couldn't they find him on their travels, then? They thought hard about all Cordelius had taught them about astral traveling and Zeb scanned all the programs they had on the subject.

"The only possible reason I can find is if they are somewhere and a barrier has been put around the planet to stop any energy entering it," said Zeb.

Samuel was now very worried. Up to now they'd been able to travel wherever they wanted and had visited many planets, but if Cordelius was somewhere that a barrier had been placed around to stop energy entering, then they were probably in great danger.

"If there is a barrier around the planet they are on, then how did they get through it?" asked Angelico.

"Doug was supposed to find the porthole that he arrived through from planet Tirleen. I wonder if it shifted," said Samuel.

Their knowledge of portholes was similar to Governor Brent's: very limited. Could portholes go to places where barriers were put around and if so, could they get out through that porthole or would it close up?

"You do realize we are forgetting everything that Cordelius has taught us, don't you?" said Zeb as he realized the energy was dropping in the sanctuary due to all the negative vibes from them.

Samuel had felt it too. Negative thoughts would not help Cordelius and the others. They all had to think positive and ask the people who were always in their lives and who they should have thought of straightaway. The angels!

"We will all channel and ask the angels what has happened and how we can help," said Samuel as he changed the music to one that would raise the vibrations and enable them all to reach the ninth plane and communicate with the angels.

Chapter 21

Space to Planet Placillon to Planet Tirleen

Captain Pren yawned. Why couldn't they find another planet? He knew they were out there, as Zut had told him in confidence that other planets existed. He wouldn't say how he knew, just that they were there and that was his mission. To find one! They had been searching for years for something called portholes. Apparently it was a way of getting to other planets and different times.

It was all a bit strange to Pren. He may be the captain of the Searchers, but before this he had never heard of portholes. For some reason he didn't understand, they had never been taught about them. Although Zut had told him to find one, he was also told not to tell any of the other crew that was what they were looking for, or even that they existed. It seemed very odd that no one else must know about them, but one did not argue with Zut!

He only had thirteen years left as Captain of the Searchers. At 85 years of age you were called a wizend and your position was filled with someone younger. He'd been furious to hear that he had lost his title as Wiron Leader and that not only was it taken by a twelve-year-old, but a female at that! Zut had said she was to become a Searcher when she joined the Planet Force and he retired and may possibly be made captain straight away. A female as captain! He couldn't believe such a thing was to happen. Females were never made Searchers and as for captain at twenty-five, well, that was totally unheard of!

He was so busy fuming at the thought of Ashtez becoming Captain of the Searchers that he was totally unprepared when the controls started to flicker madly and the ship rocketed violently from side to side. Everybody aboard panicked. What was happening? Although they were safely secured with their harnesses in their seats, their bodies were thrown about so much that they feared they would break all their bones and die. Their screams got louder and louder as the ship spun around and around, totally out of control. Then there was a violent bump and the ship was still, but they were in total darkness.

Pren took control straight away. Although his head was still whizzing about, he felt for the switches on the panel and found the emergency lighting, to his relief when he pressed it the ship lit up.

"Is everyone all right?" he shouted out.

He heard confirmation from most of the crew, but amongst it were a few moans. Pren undid his harness and got out of his seat. He looked around at the crew. A few of them were obviously dead and some badly injured, but the rest looked all right.

"Take the injured and the dead to the laser room, the programmer can do his job and then they'll be back with us," he commanded.

The dead and injured were taken away and Pren looked at the screen to see where they were. He couldn't believe what he was seeing! The sight was awe inspiring. So beautiful and relaxing. He'd finally found another planet! At long last he'd realized his dream and found another planet! They must have gone through one of those portholes that Zut had talked about. After nearly fifty years they had finally found a porthole and another planet. Zut was right, portholes and other planets did exist. Their leader was extremely clever!

He wondered how Zut knew about such things and why they weren't taught about it at cerebrumadrome? This sight was so beautiful, the rest of Tirleen should know about it! The crew joined him and gazed out at the planet they had landed on. They had never before seen such wonderful colours. The rocks were different shades of blue and the ground was such an amazing sight. They watched as the purple ground shimmered and changed from pink to yellow, to grey and then back to purple.

"This is amazing, isn't it?" said Pren, his eyes getting bigger and his body filling with excitement.

They must get some samples of this ground for Zut to see. He wondered if there was any life force here and if it was safe to leave the ship. He scanned the details on his screen. They could breathe if they left the ship, but did they need to take their wiring shields with them for protection.? He decided that as they had no idea what they would meet or experience then it was best if they all put wiring suits on as well as carry their wiring shields. They would be protected and, if attacked, their attackers would get the shock of their lives.

The laser programmer had done his job well. All the crew were back and in one piece. They listened in trepidation as Pren said they were leaving the ship to take samples and see if any life existed on this planet. After all this time on the ship and never finding anything, they had all relaxed and forgotten how dangerous a Searcher's job could be.

Relief ran through them when Pren ordered them all to don wiring suits as well as carry a wiring shield. They had forgotten about the wiring suits their leader had designed. Nothing could touch them once they had those on. Anyone that attempted to harm them was sent an electric charge that sent them flying and knocked them unconscious, and at the same time also affected the weapon they were using by sending its charge back to themselves, doubling the blow they received and perhaps even killing them!

Excitedly they all left the ship, knowing that not only were they entering a new world, but also that they were quite safe. It felt strange standing on the ground as it rippled and changed colors. Occasionally it felt as if they were going to sink into the ground, but then it would feel solid again. They took some samples of the different coloured ground, waiting for it to change and take a new color each time. Pren then decided they would try and get a sample of the beautiful blue rocks.

They waited as he used his laser knife to cut through it and take a large piece. Just as he was putting it in the container, blue liquid from the cut area squirted out and hit him in the face. He gasped in shock and then watched as it poured out of the rock and ran all over him and down his suit. As it touched his wiring suit, the liquid shot back, making it look like tiny blue stars were exploding.

"Wow! Did you see that?" Pren said excitedly to his crew. "It looks like the rock's bleeding. Does that mean it's alive?"

The crew quickly joined Pren and all cut into the rocks with their laser knives and watched in amazement as the liquid poured out then exploded into stars as it touched their suits. They were laughing so much that they did not notice the group of people who had surrounded them!

"Leave the Spectreeth alone," boomed a deep voice.

Pren jumped in shock and whirled around just in time to see something coming out of the aliens abdomens. It was shooting toward him and the rest of the crew, who had stopped laughing and were now looking terrified as they saw the aliens.

As the elastic shooting out of the Placillions' umbilicus touched the wiring suits, it sizzled and whirled back toward its owner and then wrapped itself around them. The Placillions screamed in agony as they found themselves tightly encased in their own elastic. This had never happened before. Now they were terrified! Who were these aliens that had invaded their planet? They had already started destroying the Spectreeths and were even enjoying torturing them.

Pren stared at Bontril and the rest of the Placillions. He was thankful he'd decided to don the wiring suits. They never expected to meet life force such as these aliens. He couldn't believe his luck. Zut would be so pleased with him. They'd taken some samples from this strange planet and now they had captured some life form. What would Zut make of these people when he returned with them?

He wondered what else lay on this planet. It was very exciting so far; they couldn't just flee with the samples and the prisoners. There was bound to be more wonderful and exciting treasures on this planet that they could take back with them. Pren decided they would explore further.

"Take me to your leader," he demanded.

"I am the leader," said Bontril, shaking with fear.

He was trying to work out how their elastic had rebounded and encased all of them so tightly. It was agony. Now he knew what their prisoners experienced when they caught them. He hoped these aliens did not know how to do telepathic mind torture as well. He'd seen how their prisoners suffered when they used it on them!

"Take me to your headquarters then and don't try anything else. That would be very stupid. We are far more powerful than you," said Pren, who was now enjoying himself.

This was what he'd trained for and after almost fifty years they'd finally found another planet and life force. Now he needed to find out as much as possible and take it all back to Zut.

Bontril led them toward their headquarters. As they sank into the ground, Pren started to panic. What trick were these people playing now? To his relief he found he could breathe as he became completely engulfed underneath the ground. He stared in amazement as they stopped in a large room. The walls seemed to be the same as those shimmering blue rocks. There didn't seem to be any doors or way of leaving the room. He tried not to let the aliens see he was panicking. They had to realize that *they* were the prisoners, not him and his crew.

"Remember, don't try any tricks. Our suits will shock you if you do," he said, hoping his voice wasn't quivering.

Suddenly, as if from nowhere, more of the aliens appeared. It was if they had glided through the rocky walls.

"Careful!" said Bontril telepathically as his fellow Placillions stared at their leader and the others encased in their own elastic. They were all confused and frightened, wondering how someone had managed to use their own elastic defense against them.

Pren started to tell them his demands, but none of the Placillions heard him as they telepathically spoke to each other. Bontril told them to use their powers to send mind torture to their attackers. The Placillions all stared at Pren and his crew and concentrated hard.

Pren stopped speaking as he realized the aliens silver eyes were growing and glowing. He signalled to his crew to get their wiring shields ready to use. The aliens were up to something, but he didn't know what. The crew were taut with tension, their fingers touching the control panel, ready to fire their wiring shield as soon as the aliens tried anything. The aliens didn't move. They just kept staring at Pren and his crew. It was very unnerving and they felt very uncomfortable and also a little strange.

There was a loud *clang* as all the shields fell to the floor, then a thumping sound as Pren and his crew followed. Pren stared, because that was all he could do. He had no feeling in his body at all and didn't even know if he still had one. He realized he could think, so must still have a brain, but where it was he did not know. Perhaps he didn't have a head, either.

"We are quite safe now," said Bontril, then turned to one of the other Placillions and ordered him to cut them free.

Pren's eyes widened as one of the aliens used his razor finger to cut the elastic from those encased in it. These were very strange people indeed and obviously more intelligent than he had thought. Now they were the prisoners and all the elation of discovering a new planet and capturing aliens had turned to despair. They were all doomed; he knew that much. He would never know the exhilaration of being praised by Zut and recognized as a hero and the first pioneer to discover a new world and take samples and alien prisoners back for Zut. Still, he thought, at least it wasn't painful being a prisoner. They had no bodies, just eyes. Perhaps they would just remain as a pair of eyes with a brain somewhere that allowed them to think.

"I am going to ask you some questions and now you had better tell me the truth or else you'll find out that we can be just as ruthless," said Bontril, his eyes still staring at Pren.

Pren wondered how he could answer questions with just a pair of eyes? Was he supposed to blink, or what?

"You will nod your head that you've understood the question," continued Bontril.

Pren suddenly found himself rapidly nodding a head he didn't think existed.

"Good. Then I will allow you to speak."

Pren struggled to open his mouth to speak, but found it was stuck as if they'd glued it together. How could he speak with his lips glued?

"Ouch!" he screamed, as it felt like a razor had cut through and freed his lips.

The Placillions did not react, just kept staring at Pren and the crew.

"Have you come to rescue the rest of your people?" said Bontril.

"What other...?" Pren got no further as he suddenly realized he had toes and they were being cut off with a razor! "Aaarrh!" his screams rang loudly around the room.

The rest of the Tirleens were terrified. What was happening to their captain? As far as they knew they only had eyes and a brain floating around somewhere, but Captain Pren appeared to still have his body because they could hear his screams. They all realized at once that they could hear. That must mean they still had their ears! At this precise moment in time as they listened to Pren's screams as the Placillions tortured him, they all wished their ears had disappeared along with the rest of their bodies!

Chapter 22
Escape Through the Mind

Doug was totally unaware that Captain Pren and some other Tirleens were also on the planet and were prisoners in another room. It was lucky they could not hear Pren's screams, as Cordelius was totally relaxed as he channeled with the angels. He had raised the energy in their room and now Doug and the others were feeling quite positive and certain that Cordelius would get help from the angels and show them how to escape.

Cordelius listened as the angel he was communicating with told him that the mind was very powerful and if you believed and concentrated enough then it was possible to use it to do anything you wished to. They were to use the power of their minds to escape from their prison. The Placillions had used their minds to take them to this area, so they just had to use it to get out.

Cordelius thanked the angel and came down from the ninth plane and grounded himself. He puzzled over what the angel had said. How could their minds help them escape? The walls had no way out, the aliens had just drifted in and out of them. He looked at Doug and Vonick, who were waiting expectantly and hopeful that the angels had given Cordelius the answer to how they could escape.

"We have to use our minds. They are very powerful and if we believe enough we will be free from this room," Cordelius said.

He watched as Doug and the others puzzled over this answer. The energy in the room started to drop as they struggled to understand how their minds could free them from this predicament.

"Doug, do you trust the angels? It was you who Archangel Gabriel appeared to. Where has your faith gone to?" said Cordelius.

He had to raise their energy to a very strong positive level. He too was puzzled by the answers, but knew he wouldn't have been given it unless the angel knew it would help them all.

"You are right. If they have told you we must use our minds then we must think how they want us to use them," said Doug.

Vonick realized they had no other way of escaping from this room, so if the angel had told them to use their mind then he must think how it could help them.

"We just sank through the ground when were captured and yet we could still breathe," said Cordelius as he tried to puzzle the answer out.

"Yes, and the aliens just appeared through the walls and left the same way. So there has to be a way for all of us to do the same and get back to the surface," said Vonick, feeling more positive about the situation. They had got here somehow, so they would be able to get out.

"How can we use our minds to walk through walls, Cordelius?" asked Doug.

"We tell ourselves we can do it!" said Cordelius, suddenly realizing what the angel had meant.

It was possible to move objects with the mind if you concentrated and sent enough energy to it, so you must be able to tell yourself to walk through walls. Surely it was possible? But was it? He realized he was questioning the angels and pushed the last negative thought out of his mind. It was going to be possible. The angels had said so.

"We need to meditate and raise our energy high enough to convince ourselves we can do whatever we tell our mind to do," Cordelius told them. He was positive they could do it, but looking at the rest of the laser jet crew he could see them wondering if it would work.

Vonick looked at his crew and took command of the situation. "Men, if Cordelius's angels say it is possible, then I can assure you it will be. For the moment Cordelius is in charge and we are to follow his instructions implicitly. Is that understood?"

The men nodded. If their leader thought it was possible, then it was. He had never let them down before. Cordelius wished they had some music to help raise the energy, but since they hadn't then they would all have to improvise. Doug, Vonick and the rest of the laser jet crew were all surprised at how relaxed they felt as they followed Cordelius's instructions and listened as he told them how to open their chakras.

He started talking them through a mind journey, and to their surprise they found themselves following him and could see where they were going. In their mind he took them through the walls made of rock and they found themselves just slipping through them. They then rose up through the layers until they were in the purple sand and went through each of its layers: pink, yellow and grey. Then, with a feeling of great joy, they found themselves on top and looking at the planet. They looked around in wonder and wished they could stay there, but Cordelius then brought their mind travel back to the beginning and they found themselves in the room again, still prisoners.

"That was wonderful," said Vonick as he opened his eyes. "I didn't know meditation could be so relaxing and yet feel so exhilarating at the same time."

Cordelius smiled. He had got them this far, now he needed to keep their energy high and their minds powerful enough to convince them that they could all walk through the rocks and float up to the surface.

Doug and the others all felt a little strange at first as Cordelius got them to repeatedly say the word "Om" aloud, but strangely enough the longer they all made the sound, the more confident they felt. They could make that same journey exactly as they did in their minds.

"Vonick, you go first with your men. I will go last in case anyone doubts they can do it," said Cordelius.

It was good to see how positive the men were and the energy in the room felt fantastic. Thank goodness he remembered that the word "Om" could raise the energy as much as music.

"Keep concentrating, Vonick, and telling yourself you can do it. Don't hesitate or think otherwise," he told Vonick.

Vonick got up and ordered his men to follow him without thinking or questioning. He walked to the wall and Doug blinked as Vonick just disappeared through it. He watched as one by one his men followed, until there was only Garm remaining. Garm walked toward the wall and bounced backward!

"Ouch!" he yelled.

Cordelius tried not to panic. Everything was going so well up to now. Why was there always one who doubted things? He chastised himself as he realized that he had doubted the angels were with them when they'd got captured, so it was easy enough to do.

"Doug, you go next. I will help Garm through."

Doug concentrated on walking through the wall and tried not to allow his mind to think otherwise. He found himself gazing at the inside of the blue rocks, and looking in wonder at the blue liquid running all around. He felt calmer and calmer. Suddenly he was rising up, up, up and out onto the surface where Vonick and his crew, apart from Garm, were waiting and looking very pleased with themselves.

"We did it!" said Vonick. They had done the impossible; they had not only walked through a wall, but had risen up to the surface and all just by telling their minds it was possible.

If they got out of here alive he was going to visit Cordelius's White Light Sanctuary and learn more about meditation. Suddenly he realized he'd said "if." Of course they were going to escape. They had angels helping them!

"You can do it, Garm," said Cordelius, still down below. "We are going to start by repeating the word "Om" and then you are going to hold on to me and we are going through that wall and up to the surface to join the others."

Garm's body relaxed as he continued saying "Om" with Cordelius. Cordelius waited until he could see that Garm was in a dreamlike state, then took hold of his arm and quickly pulled him through the wall before he could think that it wasn't going to be possible.

Garm opened his eyes and looked around. He was on top of the surface with the rest of the men! He hadn't a clue how it had happened, but he was free! The angels were right, the mind was a very powerful thing. They had walked through walls and flew up in the air. He had wondered how Cordelius was going to help on this rescue mission as he wasn't used to fighting or defending himself, but he had used the most powerful weapon of all: their minds!

Now they were all on the surface and free Vonick took command once again. "Come on, let's hurry. We have to find where we entered the planet and see if the porthole is still there," he said.

They all hurried along the shimmering ground, not noticing or caring how beautiful it was as it changed colors. They were anxious to leave this planet as quickly as possible. They didn't want to risk getting caught again. The Placillions would surely kill them next time.

As they reached the area they arrived on, they all stopped and stood as if in a trance. There in front of them was an enormous spaceship! That hadn't been there when they fell through the porthole. Cordelius trembled. Were there more aliens on board that spaceship and where had it came from?

Vonick got his laser pin ready to fire and walked toward the spaceship. The others held back, not knowing whether to follow or wait for Vonick to order them to. Vonick reached the spaceship door and touched it. Instantly it opened. He jumped back in surprise and then quickly gestured to the others to follow him. This was their way out of this terrible planet and he would kill its occupants if necessary.

Doug and Cordelius stayed well behind the laser jet crew. All the fighters had weapons to defend themselves with, whereas they had nothing. Apart from Cordelius's angels, of course! Vonick touched a panel on the wall and the ship closed its door. Quietly they crept around and looked all through the ship. It appeared to be empty.

"This looks very similar to the spaceships the Searchers on

Tirleen used," said Doug. He had gotten over his fear as he realized the ship was empty and they were quite safe.

"Can you fly it?" asked Cordelius.

"I don't think so. I may know how some of the programs work, though," Doug replied as he looked at all the panels. He looked at Vonick. "Can't you fly it? You fly the laser jets."

Vonick looked at all the panels, too. This ship was miles bigger than their small laser jets with just a few panels to control. "If we all work together we may be able to fly it," he said, looking at his crew hopefully. "Doug, you used to work on the programs, so whilst we are checking how to take off, you see what you know about them."

"What shall I do?" said Cordelius.

"Pray!" said Vonick as he sat in the captain's seat and buckled the harness up.

Chapter 23

Planet Tirleen
Sirleen Sees the Light

Anjoy was scared. Nothing was going as God had planned. Sirleen refused to help them, and Zut, the leader, did not even believe that they were real. Despite this he was obviously very afraid of them as his guards had been ordered to capture the children and their families, which is why most of them were hiding in these tunnels. The missing children and their families had been captured whilst they were all fleeing and were now in those awful living tubes.

It distressed Anjoy so much to think of her friends in those awful tubes that she had stopped talking to God for several days now. She was really angry with him. Why had he sent them back here? They were happy in heaven. Down here they might be with their parents, but they also endured pain, fear and loneliness. Yes, loneliness! She thought it was very lonely without God putting his arms around them and comforting them.

The planet was getting darker as more of the dark angels took over and were slowly suffocating everyone and lowering the energy. Everyone's spirits were now very low. Soon the energy would be so low that anger would take over and the destruction would begin.

Anjoy didn't realize it was the dark angels that were causing her to feel pain and sorrow and making her lose her trust in God. God had been trying to talk to her for days, but the negative energy all around had blocked her ears. He felt her pain, too, and hoped the rescuers would get all his "miracles" out before the dark angels smothered the planet and he lost them.

At their leader's drome, Zut was gleefully looking at the new Lens and Gaming drome programs. He was really pleased he had thought about it as he watched the figures for lens use continually rise in front of his eyes. The figures for the Galiquer may have dropped since the Lens and Gaming drome opened, but these figures were ten times more than the Galiquer had ever taken in a night.

Everybody was addicted to it! Even the adults and the wizends were going there, which was good, as they hadn't figured out how to use the lenses, unlike the children. This meant they were continually playing the lenses to try and beat them. The children, on the other hand, just played them for pleasure, so the tirns were rolling in.

Zut laughed to himself as he recalled that thing called Anjoy telling him that God was angry with everyone for getting drunk, including the children. Well, if he had existed, he couldn't complain now. They were all gambling instead!

He pushed the thought of those things out of his mind. Just the image of them made him really angry. He'd gotten control of his planet back now as he'd upped the subliminal programming. He was slightly worried that some of the stronger brains were still resisting and wondering if this "God" did exist.

Thankfully, the Planet Force guards had caught some of the "angel children" and their families, as well as a few more Faith Believers, and they were all now in living tubes on display to show the rest of his people how ruthless he could be.

As for this God, well, nobody was as intelligent as he was. He was well aware that portholes existed and that some of his people had found them and had escaped through them. This was why he had Searchers always looking for these other planets and new life. Apart from himself and Sirleen, Captain Pren was one of the few people who were privileged to know about portholes.

Pren was due back any time now, so he hoped that this time they had finally found one of the portholes. There had been no contact from him for a while now, but sometimes that happened, or perhaps he'd struck lucky for once and finally flown into a porthole. It irked Zut that other people on his planet had found them and used them to escape and yet he, the most intelligent of all people, could never find one. He continually looked and yet up to now he hadn't felt any different energy around the planet.

He turned his attention back to figures for the Lens and Gaming drome, but was interrupted as Sirleen's face appeared on the screen.

"What do you want, Sirleen?" he snapped. "I'm busy."

"I need to see you urgently."

"Well, it had better be important then," said Zut as he flicked Sirleen's face off the screen to get his lens figures back.

Sirleen teleported into Zut's quarters. He looked worried and tense and it made Zut feel edgy. *What was wrong now?* he thought.

"The sky is getting darker by the minute. Why haven't you changed the programs to bring the light back in? Aren't you able to?" said Sirleen, risking Zut's anger as he questioned his ability to program the light.

Zut's eyes darkened as the anger rose in his body.

"How dare you question my ability to program the light. I've just been too busy creating other programs, that's all."

"Like the Lens Room, to make more tirns, I suppose?" snapped Sirleen. He hadn't a clue where this anger in him was coming from, but it seemed to be making him very brave. Never before had he argued with Zut in such a way.

"I run this planet, not you!" said Zut, who was now practically exploding with anger. "Perhaps I've decided to keep the planet dark for a while because the people don't deserve the light after questioning who was in charge of them."

"Perhaps you don't know how to get rid of the darkness," said Sirleen with a smirk on his face. He was really enjoying himself. He hadn't a clue what was going on, but it felt good to feel so angry for once. It gave him the courage to stand up to Zut!

He had found it felt good to think for himself since he had worked out that Zut was subliminally programming everyone and controlling all their thoughts. He had come across the subliminal program quite by chance. Every day at precisely the 1,000th wixon, a sound was heard. As this was normally when everyone was sleeping, nobody had realized what was happening, because this was when the subliminal messages were fed into their thoughts.

Sirleen had been woken yet again by one of those angel visions and before he'd gone to sleep again he had heard the sound, then Zut's voice quietly and hypnotically sending messages to all their brains. As he realized what was happening he blocked his ears to avoid hearing Zut's voice. Now every night when he slept, he kept his ears well blocked. It felt good when he woke up each day because now he was in control of his own mind!

The angel vision, or perhaps programs, were a regular occurrence, and Sirleen was starting to wonder if they were real or not. The last time the angel had appeared, he had been told to look for the programs the Faith Believers held and were safely hidden somewhere on the planet. This would tell him all about God and the angels and prove that they existed.

Zincon's death had been quite disturbing. He had never seen anyone die before two hundred and fifty. They were always repaired. He knew it had shocked Zut, too. Zut had been hoping to torture Zincon then place him on display in the living tubes, but he'd got his revenge by placing Zincon's family in them instead. Sirleen could still see Zincon smiling as his body drifted away, surrounded by those angels or "programs." Zut was still trying to work out how he'd escaped. He still wasn't sure if Zincon had programmed it and somehow he was still alive on the planet, hiding somewhere with the things he'd programmed.

Sirleen, on the other hand, wasn't so sure now that he could think for himself. He had started searching the planet for the programs the angel vision had spoken about, but so far hadn't found any. He had tried searching Zincon's quarters, but it was nowhere to be found in there. Perhaps it was in one of the tunnels they had used for their secret meetings? That was where he must start looking next. For the moment, however, he felt that Zut needed to answer some questions, such as why was the light not coming in? It felt good seeing Zut so rattled!

He left Zut still seething and very angry. Sirleen wondered if he had gone too far. He was their leader after all and quite capable of doing anything, even placing the Spirit Master in a living tube if he realized he wasn't subliminally controlling him anymore.

Instead of teleporting or using the flier, Sirleen decided to walk around the planet as he looked for the programs, knowing he'd be quite safe as people normally teleported or used the flier all the time so would not be seen. He needed to decide which tunnel to start searching first and hoped the quietness would help him think. He had forgotten about the darkness over the planet and the heavy atmosphere was making his brain foggy. It felt like he was out of control again. All he could feel was anger, especially at Zut. How dare one person control all of them and how dare he block out their light!

He looked at the faces of the people in the living tubes as they stared at him. They seemed to be everywhere he walked and their eyes looked angry as he stared back at them. It was almost as if they could think and were blaming him for their being in the tubes.

This puzzled him as he walked past more and more of them. Firstly, Zut had placed them in the tubes, and secondly they were just living in there. How could they…? He stopped and stared hard as he looked at one of the "angel children." Broocen was staring back at him and his eyes were pleading with him. There was no anger in them, just pleading, and he was sure that he saw a tear forming in Broocen's eyes. Was it possible Zincon still could control his programs in a living tube? Surely not?

Sirleen wiped his face and realized he was crying, too. He had never cried before! What was happening here? Somehow he felt this child's pain and his tears were really upsetting him because now tears were pouring down Broocen's face. Sirleen instinctively put his hand on the living tube to try and soothe Broocen. As Broocen placed his hand on the glass to match Sirleen's, a warm feeling spread throughout his body. The word "love" instantly came into his mind.

Broocen smiled. *God was right*, he thought to himself. Someone was going to help them. At last someone else was experiencing God's love! Surely if the Spirit Master realized that God did exist then he could convince the rest of the planet, too?

Broocen had found it hard when Anjoy had stopped coming to reassure him that God would send help and free him. He didn't realize that the living tubes were the one place they were safe from the negative energy the dark angels were placing over the planet, which was why he could still hear and talk to God, whereas Anjoy had blocked his voice out.

"It's up to you for the moment," God said to Broocen.

"What do I have to do? I am trapped."

"Just keep smiling and sending my love out to the Spirit Master. It will raise his energy and give him the strength to help and when my angels appear to him again he may finally realize that they are real."

Broocen kept smiling and prayed hard that Sirleen wouldn't move away. It seemed to be working because Sirleen's face was now smiling back and seemed to be sending love back to Broocen. He could feel his hands tingling and his heart felt warm. God was right. The Spirit Master had felt his love. Soon they would all be safe and he prayed that when they were free that God would take him back to heaven to be with him once again and let him feel his love.

Sirleen was enjoying the love that was filling his body. It felt good; he felt alive. Somehow he had to help all of these people trapped in the tubes. Zut had no right trapping people. So what if they did believe in this God, if it made then feel as good as he was right now, then he could understand why they'd disobeyed Zut. This love feeling was very powerful. He felt he could fight anyone—even Zut!

Reluctantly he took his hand away from the tube, so was relieved when the warm feeling stayed with him. He waved to Broocen as he strode off toward the tunnels. Somehow he would find a way to help those poor people.

The bright lights and the noise from the Lens and Gaming drome seemed to be the only light on their planet, and as Sirleen passed it to enter one of the tunnels he wondered if Ashtez was in there. *Now she would be capable of matching Zut's brains,* he thought to himself as his eyes adjusted to the darkness of the tunnels. The trouble was he'd convinced her that this God didn't exist and now he found himself questioning all he'd taught her and the rest of the planet.

She was still being subliminally controlled by Zut. If he could find a way to make her block her ears, then perhaps she could help break all Zut's programs so that the rest of the planet would think for themselves and perhaps stop Zut from ruling them. The problem was Ashtez and Hurlen now lived with their wizends, and whereas he felt that Edril was a secret Faith Believer, he knew that Epsone hated them. If Ashtez started questioning Zut's orders and wondering if Anjoy was really alive, then Epsone would inform Zut, and Ashtez would quickly be placed in a living tube.

The more Sirleen thought of helping the people in the living tubes and trying to find a way to block Ashtez's ears, the more he realized that perhaps God did exist.

He could almost hear a voice talking in his ears. His ears kept ringing, but he could still quite clearly hear someone saying "help them."

His legs were feeling weary after all the walking, so he decided to sit down and rest a while. He wasn't used to walking and he had covered quite a distance so far. He hoped he didn't get lost in the tunnels.

He found his eyes closing and then he was in a strange room. It was very bright and the music was so peaceful. There was a young girl and two men were holding her hands and they were all floating around the room from one corner to the other. They seemed so real as they stared at him.

"It is just another traveler," said one of the men as he floated past him.

"He will not harm you. We always protect ourselves before we travel and if you get frightened you just go back to your body," said the other man.

How strange, thought Sirleen, wondering who the traveler was as the people suddenly disappeared into bodies the same as the ones that had been floating around. He hadn't noticed the still bodies before, but now he watched as their doubles disappeared through the top of their heads and they became one and started moving around.

"You did well, Fiona. Tomorrow we will travel around our city," said Samuel.

"And then can I go to Tirleen and see if my father has rescued the angel children," she said excitedly.

"Yes, and we will come with you. We have tried searching for Cordelius and the rest of the rescue mission, but so far have not found them. We are as anxious as you to know what is going on," said Samuel.

Sirleen was fascinated. Who were these strange people and why were they talking about Tirleen? How did they know about Tirleen? He carried on listening to their conversations. The one called Samuel was mentioning portholes. How did they know about such things? Zut had kept them a secret and yet he was talking as if they knew all about them and had been used by lots of people, including this girl's father.

Sirleen was sure this man had said that Doug, her father, had escaped from Tirleen through one. Was that possible? The population hadn't changed, nobody was unaccounted for. He heard the name Rone mentioned. Rone was one of the Faith Believers in the living tubes. How did they know about him?

A loud snore made Sirleen jump and he realized it was himself. He opened his eyes and realized he had been dreaming. Dreaming was something new to him. Up to now they had been unable to dream. Sometimes he quite enjoyed his dreams, the pleasant ones, of course, but then some of them were quite terrifying. He remembered the one from the other night when he watched a man being tortured by strange beings with enormous umbilicus. That was definitely not caused by too many mince pies, because Given was a long way off.

He tried to recall the dream he'd just had. Since he had stopped being controlled by Zut and started dreaming, he had taken to writing them down every day. Surely they must mean something since there seemed to be a pattern with them. The name Doug came up several times. Who was he? Rone, he knew was on the planet. He wondered if he could communicate with Rone somehow. He had felt love from that child, so perhaps there was a way to talk to them.

Now he had to get out of the tunnels before he got lost, but which way should he turn: left or right? A voice in his ears said "right," so he instinctively went that way. He hoped it wasn't too far to go, as he was shattered. When he got out he would find the nearest teleport and use it!

A sobbing noise was coming from somewhere. Sirleen stopped and listened. Was someone else in this tunnel with him? Quietly he walked towards the noise and as it got louder he realized it was children that were sobbing and adults voices were talking as they tried to soothe them. He turned a corner and panic ensued as the sobs turned to screams and the adults joined in. They all rushed toward him. He was terrified. There were a lot of them and they could easily harm him.

"Stop!" he screamed as loudly as he could.

Everybody stopped!

"Be careful," screamed Odraine. "He could have the Planet Force guards with him.

Sirleen realized it was the "angel children" and their parents, as well as other Faith Believers.

"I do not want to harm you," he said.

"You mightn't, but the Planet Force guards will. When are they going to realize that God has sent our children back to prove that he does exist?" sobbed Viola.

She hated living in the tunnels. She may have her beloved Anjoy back, but she had lost her other two children, Ashtez and Hurlen. They would have nothing to do with them and especially not with Anjoy. Her wizend, Edril, visited regularly and told her how they were, but she couldn't send any messages back as that would put Edril in danger.

“I believe that God exists,” said Sirleen.

As everybody gasped, he realized how wonderful he felt. He had actually said aloud that God existed. Now where had that thought come from? Yet he did feel that God existed, but for the moment nobody else must know that he felt that way. He couldn’t help these people if Zut found out he was now a Faith Believer!

“It’s a trick,” yelled Odraine. Everybody huddled together as they waited for the Planet Force guards to appear.

Sirleen realized they were all very scared of him and wondered how he could convince them he really did believe in God and wanted to help not harm them.

“Kneel and pray,” said a voice in his head.

How do I pray, he thought.

“Just talk to me. It’s God,” said the voice.

“God, is it you that is talking in my ears?” said Sirleen in his mind.

“Yes, now pray and they will follow,” said God.

Sirleen looked at the frightened people and got down on his knees. He remembered seeing a picture of an angel on his programs, praying. You put your hands together and pointed them upward and talked aloud to God.

“God, I ask that you give me strength, hope and courage to find a way to help your angel children and their families,” he said.

Everybody looked at Anjoy, who was walking toward the Spirit Master. They watched her touch his hands and look into his smiling face.

“Can you hear God talking to you?” she said in wonder.

“Yes, I can, and he has asked me to put my hands on your ears and unblock them so that you can once again hear him.”

Anjoy knelt in front of Sirleen and allowed him to place his hands on her ears. The warmth coming from them and filling her body made her feel wonderful and floaty. She could feel God hugging her and kissing her again. He was back in her life and she could feel his love and most importantly she could hear him talking to her!

“Anjoy, you must help raise the spirits on the planet. The dark angels are allowing you all to feel despondent. Soon all of you will stop believing in me.”

"No! No!" she screamed aloud. "We will never stop believing in you."

"Tell the others that Sirleen is not tricking them. He now believes in me and will help you. Listen to him."

Anjoy turned and faced everybody and told them what God had said. They all looked at her, amazed. Her face was lit up and she seemed to be shining as if there was a glow all around her body. Viola and Odraine rushed up and hugged her. If Anjoy said that God had told her to listen to Sirleen, then they must believe her. He had sent them their beloved daughter back as a gift, so now they must help her convince the rest of them that Sirleen was on their side. They could see from some of the other adults faces that they weren't sure whether to trust Sirleen or not. They couldn't blame them, after all, he was the Spirit Master and up to now he had always tried to teach them that God was a "fairy tale."

"Listen to our daughter. She is right, and Sirleen will now help us," Viola said, looking at the confused faces of the other adults.

Odraine turned toward Sirleen. He could understand why Anjoy believed him. Sirleen seemed to be glowing, too, and he could feel warmth emitting from his body. Sirleen put his hand out and placed it on Odraine's heart. Odraine sighed with pleasure. He could feel God's love; he could really feel it! Up to now, well, only since Anjoy had come back, but up to now he just knew that God must exist. How else would Anjoy and the others be alive? Now, though, now he could feel God's love. It was just amazing!

"What must be we do, Sirleen?" he asked.

"Show me how to get out of this tunnel unseen and then I think I must somehow try to get your daughter Ashtez to help us."

"Ashtez!" gasped Odraine. Now he was scared. Ashtez would never help them. Surely Sirleen realized that?

"Everybody has been and still are being subliminally controlled by Zut not to believe in God. It is done at night when they are asleep. If I can find a way to block her ears then she will start to listen to me," Sirleen told him.

Odraine walked with Sirleen, showing him a much shorter route that would take him out and near the teleport at the celestdrome. It was very dark now, so no one would see him leaving. Odraine prayed that they didn't anyhow, because now they finally all had the help they had been praying for!

Both of them tried to think how they could persuade Ashtez to keep her ears blocked at night so that she would eventually listen to Sirleen. Suddenly Odraine remembered how excited she had been at Given when she had received all the lenses she wanted. Was this the way? Through her love of gaming, could they make her block her ears?

"Edril says Ashtez practically lives in the Lens and Gaming drome. If only there was a way to make her go there at night and use something that would involve blocking her ears," Odraine said just as they reached the teleport safely. Before Sirleen left, Odraine told him a quicker and safer route so that next time he wouldn't get lost in the tunnels.

Sirleen then teleported to his quarters and quickly blocked his ears when he realized it was nearly the 1,000th wixon. He had been gone longer than he thought. No wonder he was tired. He went to bed still pondering over how he could get Ashtez to block her ears.

Chapter 24

Planet Trehf and Astral Travel to Planet Tirleen

Fiona was really excited. Today they were going to allow her to travel to Tirleen! Even though she wasn't going alone it was still thrilling. In a way she was glad that Samuel and Zeb were traveling with her, because if she saw her father and he was trapped in one of those awful living tubes, she didn't know what she would do. She would probably end up back in her body before she had found a way to help him.

She walked through the hologram of the angel, feeling lighter as the energy lifted her spirits. Not that they needed lifting today! She had finally learnt how to astral project through meditation and as she'd been taught properly, she was now going to be able to travel wherever she wanted.

When her father came back with the angel children, she was going to travel to all the different planets she had read about on her computer programs. She might even get to visit a real sea and sit on the beach!

Samuel and Zeb were waiting for her. Quickly they talked her through the meditation and soon they were all flying, or rather whizzing, through the atmosphere. Zeb had explained that when they astral traveled a long way they used speed traveling. *It was aptly named,* Fiona thought as she felt her head going dizzy as she watched everything whizzing past her eyes.

She blinked as it all slowed down and they found themselves on Tirleen in front of some of the living tubes. Fiona had told Samuel and Zeb about these and how many there were of them, but nothing had prepared them for this. Zeb was so shocked he shot straight back to his body. Samuel told Fiona not to worry, he would soon be back with them and this time he would have prepared his mind not to be shocked at the sight.

Fiona was just showing Samuel the living tube with Broocen when Zeb rejoined them. He apologized to Fiona, saying that it had never happened to him before, with all the sights he had seen, but the living tubes were worse than he was expecting. He could feel the pain and misery it caused the people trapped inside them.

They looked at Broocen and wondered how anyone could cause a child to have so much pain. The person ruling this planet must be very ruthless. They'd found it hard to believe that he had ignored God's gifts, but to do this to any child, let alone a gift from God, was just unbelievable.

Samuel blinked as Sirleen approached and stopped in front of Broocen. Where had he seen this person before? He seemed really familiar. How could they know him?

"That's that traveler," whispered Fiona, not realizing that Sirleen couldn't hear them anyhow. "He must live here. I wonder who he is?"

Sirleen put his hand on the tube against Broocen's and, despite being in their astral bodies, they could all feel God sending his love through Broocen. Sirleen now knew that he could communicate with Broocen by using telepathic thoughts. He was telling him that he had found Anjoy and the other children and with God's help they would soon free everyone. Some people from another planet were on their way to help take them all through portholes to another planet, but they hadn't arrived yet.

Broocen asked Sirleen how they were going to free all of them in the living tubes. Sirleen told him not to worry, he was sure he had finally found a way, and if Broocen prayed with all the others for his plan to work then they would soon be free.

Fiona, Samuel and Zeb left Sirleen and Broocen and traveled around the rest of Tirleen, looking for her father and the others. To their disappointment they were nowhere to be seen, so they flew back to their bodies to discuss what to do next.

Samuel and Zeb tried to hide their disappointment from Fiona. They could see how elated she was from her first "flight" and remembered how they had felt on theirs.

"Are you sure we looked everywhere for them?" Zeb asked, hoping that perhaps they were hiding somewhere Fiona had forgotten about.

"I think so, but I'll go and check dad's notes and see if there is anywhere else they could hide."

She rushed out, still full of exhilaration and anxious to look in Doug's notes and go traveling again. Now she could travel she knew she would find her father and the others. It was the most wonderful feeling she'd every experienced!

Chapter 25

Planet Tirleen
Round Two to the Spirit Master

Sirleen went to Epsone and Edril's quarters to see Ashtez. Epsone was delighted to have a visit from the Spirit Master, but was surprised when he refused a galiquon. Sirleen suddenly realized how strange this would look and told Epsone he was visiting Zut afterward, so needed a clear head to talk to him.

Epsone accepted this excuse and fetched Ashtez from her sleeping quarters. She had been busy working on a new lens program. She knew that Zut was not happy with her and Hurlen because of that stupid thing her parents called their daughter. "It" had probably ruined all her chances of being a Searcher, so she was doing all she could to find a way to impress him. She had come up with an idea for a new lens program. She wanted to show him how clever she was at programming so that she would be an asset to him.

Reluctantly she filed it away when Epsone told her the Spirit Master was visiting and had asked to see her. Although she liked the Spirit Master, she was afraid he may be trying to see if she knew where her parents were hiding with the things. She didn't want to get into his bad books as well, as he had seemed really pleased with her when she won the Wiron Leader title. She couldn't tell him where her parents were, though, because she didn't know. If she did she would readily tell him.

Epson was unwilling to leave Ashtez alone with Sirleen when he was asked. It was a great honour having the Spirit Master visit them. He hoped Sirleen wouldn't get cross with Ashtez when she told him they didn't know where Viola and Odraine were with the things. He thought that was probably why Sirleen had visited them. Why else would the great Spirit Master visit them?

He himself was ashamed of Viola and Odraine. He couldn't believe they were now Faith Believers and saying a program was their daughter sent from God. He shuddered at the word God. Just saying it made him feel ill. If ever he found out where they were hiding then he wouldn't hesitate to tell Zut. It might even get him better living quarters, too!

Ashtez patiently waited for Sirleen to speak and hoped she wasn't going to offend him when she couldn't answer his questions.

"I hear you are a regular visitor to the new Lens and Gaming drome. Our leader will be very pleased with that. If you keep it up you will soon be back in his good books and the Searcher position will be yours once again when you are old enough," he said as he smiled at her and hoped she could feel God's love as he sent it through him.

Ashtez could barely speak, she was overjoyed. She might still be able to be a Searcher! She listened intently as Sirleen told her how impressed he was with her wiring program knowledge. Perhaps she would be able to help him with a few of his programs he was having trouble with? She beamed at Sirleen and said she would be delighted to help him and when would he like her to go to his quarters?

"Why not now?" he said, before she changed her mind. He had to get her away from Epsone's prying ears. He knew he was listening to them outside, so he had to be very careful what he said.

Odraine and Edril were delighted with the news and soon Ashtez was sat in front of Sirleen's work station. Edril had left soon after as well. She wanted to tell Viola the good news that the plan was going well so far. Unfortunately she was so pleased with Sirleen's plan working that for once she was reckless and didn't bother to check if she was being followed or not!

Sirleen put the program on that the Faith Believers had given him. It was the secret one that the angel had told him to look for and would prove that God existed. Ashtez was shocked as she listened to the program. This was compelling stuff! She could see the Spirit Master had a tough task here. How was he supposed to change this program back? Somebody had obviously tampered with this and they had done a really good job of it. She herself was almost believing it!

"Very powerful, isn't it, Ashtez? So what do you think we should do?" Sirleen asked.

"They've certainly done a very good job. Zut himself couldn't program something like this. Only a Faith Believer would know how to have changed this. The angels are really beautiful, aren't they? They almost make you feel glad to be alive," she said, unable to take her eyes off the angel on the screen.

Sirleen waited for her next reaction. He knew what was going to happen! Ashtez's eyes grew wider and wider as she watched the angel become just a face and then it spoke to her. Ashtez!

"Ashtez, listen to Sirleen. Help him. God does exist. The angel children need your help."

The angel disappeared, and Sirleen tried not to smile as Ashtez turned toward him. Total disbelief was written all over her face!

"Did you see that?" she said, her eyes still the size of saucers.

"Yes," he said, trying to look grim. "It happens a lot, but I'm sure with your help we will work it out."

As it was late, he suggested to Ashtez that she sleep in his spare sleeping room and then perhaps they could do a bit of work on the program before cerebrumadrome. Ashtez readily agreed and carried on looking at the angels talking whilst Sirleen contacted Epsone to let him know what was happening. He told Epsone how pleased he was with Ashtez's help and would find it very useful if she could stay a while. The program they were working on was causing a lot of problems and if they didn't sort it out quickly then more people would become Faith Believers.

At the words "Faith Believers," Epsone readily agreed and told Sirleen to let Ashtez stay as long as he needed her. Sirleen thanked him and rejoined Ashtez. He suggested to her that they look at a few more programs before they retired. He particularly wanted her to see the "miracles" one. That was amazing and he wasn't sure what they could do with it.

Ashtez watched all of God's miracles performed by a man called Jesus. She recalled that at Given they mocked that name, but that was a baby and yet here he was as a grown man performing miracles. She never thought of him as a grown man.

"Wow!" she said, looking at Sirleen. "This one is definitely powerful stuff. I just found myself thinking that man Jesus was real!"

"It's easily done. It has happened to me many times," he said, smiling at her.

Ashtez was stunned. No wonder she had found herself believing this man was real. If it had happened to the Spirit Master, then nobody else who watched this program stood a chance. They would all be taken in. This programmer was good, really good. She would like to meet him, even if he was a Faith Believer. His knowledge of programs was obviously even greater than Zut's!

Sirleen showed her to the sleeping quarters and, to her surprise, he handed her some plugs for her ears. He explained that this programmer had somehow found a way of making noises at night to try and disturb his sleep. He thought it was probably to make him unable to concentrate on the program properly, knowing that if he was tired he would never break any of his programs.

Ashtez put the plugs in her ears. She didn't want to be tired in the morning. The Spirit Master needed her help! If Zut heard how clever she had been in helping him and she kept up her visits to the Lens Room then he might become proud of her once again.

She was mesmerized as she watched the angels floating all around her. She touched one of their wings and the feathers felt soft and warm. She allowed them to hold her and lift her up high into the sky until she found herself standing on some shiny white marble steps. The angels told her it was the kingdom of heaven and she was very welcome to enter it.

Ashtez couldn't wait. The singing and the music coming from

inside was beautiful. She wanted to cry, but with joy. She wanted to be in there with whoever was making that wonderful sound. She found herself floating and looking at what seemed to be thousands of angels, all singing. Now she knew who was making this beautiful music.

A deep voice spoke her name and she looked at God. He told her that she must help her parents and her sister. It was only her knowledge that was going to free everyone and bring love and light back to the planet.

Ashtez found herself in her bed and awake as she repeatedly said the words "love and light" over and over again. She suddenly realized what she was doing and laughed. She didn't know why she felt so happy, but she did. She felt really good! It didn't matter if she was still thinking of that program, which was why she had dreamt of angels. It made her feel so good. She just didn't care. It was a good dream. She didn't realize that was the first time she had dreamt, having never been allowed to before. She was floating with happiness.

Sirleen noticed the difference in Ashtez straightaway. He hated deceiving her into thinking she was getting back into Zut's good books, but the sooner she found out how evil he was, the sooner she would use her wiring knowledge to help them all.

Ashtez watched some more programs showing Jesus doing more of his miracles. When an angel appeared on the screen, she felt compelled to put her hand on it to see if the feathers felt the same. She was quite disappointed just to feel the flat, cold screen. Then to her joy, the angel grew until it was just a face again and started talking to her personally once more.

"Soon you will always feel our love, but you must help. That is all that we ask of you. Help the others, please."

"How strange," she said to Sirleen. "The programmer somehow knows I am helping you, yet he wants me to help. Is he trying to make me into a Faith Believer?"

"Possibly," said Sirleen, smiling.

"Well, don't worry, Sirleen. I am quite strong. That won't happen."

"I am sure he will keep on trying, so let's see what he has to say after cerebrumadrome," said Sirleen, showing her to the teleport.

Ashtez found it hard to concentrate at cerebrumadrome. She was constantly drifting off and thinking of the angels singing and how soft they felt. She still experienced a warm glow every time she thought of it. Her head shook as she was zapped once again through the wires in her fourth lobe for not concentrating on the program she was receiving. Desperately she tried to let the information flow through the wires, but she kept thinking of the angels and stroking their feathers. Zap after zap went through her wires. Apart from the pain, she now felt quite dizzy.

She was glad when the sixty wixons were over and she teleported back into Sirleen's quarters. She was still in a daze and was glad to be sat in front of his programs, looking at the angels. Somehow it seemed to soothe her head and she allowed her mind to drift and listen to what they were saying. She didn't realize she had been watching for hours; she was totally mesmerized by it all.

"Sometimes this program seems to make sense, doesn't it?" she suddenly heard Sirleen say.

She took her eyes off the screen and looked into his smiling face. What was the Spirit Master suggesting? Was he telling her that angels and God did exist? Ashtez didn't answer him. She didn't want to say the wrong thing. What was the right thing, though? She found herself totally confused and not knowing whether the angels on the screen were right, or all that the Spirit Master had taught them was right. Anyhow, it looked like he didn't know now either.

"I have to go somewhere now. Can you carry on watching these programs for me? You might get some sudden insight into what we have to do," he said.

She nodded and almost in a trance turned her attention back to the screen, not noticing that Sirleen had left.

Sirleen teleported into the Evaporation Room. It was closed at night and always left empty, so it enabled him to use its rear exit, which wasn't far from one of the tunnels. Odraine had shown him this way the last time he visited them. They'd decided that the Celestdrome entrance wasn't really safe at night. There were too many people around there. He'd been lucky that other night, God had protected him with his angels.

He still double-checked that he hadn't been followed. He couldn't be too sure that Zut knew he was a Faith Believer now. If he ever found out and put him in a living tube, then nobody would be able to free them. Ashtez would go back to Epsone and Edril and the subliminal programming would start on her again. She was doing so well and after only one day without it. He felt sure that very soon she would listen when he told her that he, too, was now a Faith Believer and wouldn't be horrified and report him to Zut.

It was strangely quiet as he walked down the tunnels near to where everyone was hidden, and then he heard it. A child was sobbing very, very quietly. Something was very wrong and he tried to stop himself from trembling and running away in a panic. He had to find this child and help it. He remembered what the angel had told him and made his body relax so that he could really concentrate and talk to God.

"What is wrong here, God?"

"They have been captured, only Anjoy is left. Find her and hide her."

Oh no! Panic set in again as Sirleen looked all around. He was worried that he may have been followed and would also be caught. He made himself realize he was being silly. Of course he hadn't been followed. If Zut knew he was a Faith Believer, or even if he knew he had found their hiding place and hadn't told him, then he would have been tortured and placed in a living tube by now.

Very quickly Sirleen walked along, all the time listening out for the occasional sob and trying to follow it. His heart felt heavy and in pain. He could feel Anjoy's sorrow, so he must be close to her.

"Anjoy," he whispered. "It is me, Sirleen. I have come to help you. God has told me everything."

Anjoy stopped sobbing as she heard Sirleen's voice. She was so confused. Was it safe to let Sirleen help her, or would he give her up to the nasty man, Zut? She had been terrified when her mother's wizend, Epsone, had appeared, followed by the Planet Force guards. In the screaming and confusion they hadn't noticed her slip past them and hide in a very dark corner of the tunnel. She barely breathed as she watched the frightened children and adults arrested and taken away. She knew what their fate would be. Tortured, then put in a living tube. *Oh God, why aren't you helping us,* she had thought. She was so sad that it stopped her from hearing God again. Now she had to decide whether to remain safely hidden or allow Sirleen to help her.

A bright white light appeared in front of her and she put her hand up to shield her eyes. She could just make out a face. It looked like Archangel Michael, the fighter and protector of everyone. Was it him?

"Anjoy, trust Sirleen. I will guide you both to safety. Do not worry. The time is approaching when you will all be free. God is winning. The light will be back in your life soon," said the angel.

As his love reached Anjoy she relaxed and moved closer to him. It was Archangel Michael! She felt very safe now. He would protect them. Sirleen could see the white light surrounding Anjoy. He couldn't make out what it was, but he called her name softly again.

"Anjoy, come to me, let me help you, please."

Anjoy heard him and reluctantly left Archangel Michael's arms to run into Sirleen's. He wrapped them tightly around her and she realized she felt just as safe with Sirleen as she had with Archangel Michael. He kissed the top of her head and then saw Archangel Michael coming toward them.

"Come, Anjoy, we are quite safe now. We have all the protection we need to escape," he said.

Chapter 26

A New Faith Believer

Sirleen joined Ashtez at his work station. If only she knew her sister and one of God's little miracles was hiding in this drome. He hoped it wouldn't be long before he could tell her and that she would welcome her new sister into her life.

Ashtez jumped as the angel's face disappeared from the screen and Epsone's was in its place. She felt very cross with him for spoiling the peaceful time she was experiencing. What did he want anyhow?

"Ashtez you will never believe it, but we have found Viola and Odraine and all the rest of the families with those things. They are all now in living tubes," he said ecstatically. Epsone saw her frowning and realized he had stopped her from helping Sirleen. "I hope the Spirit Master doesn't mind me interrupting you whilst you work, but I felt sure you would be very pleased to hear this information!"

Sirleen's face appeared in front of Epsone. He couldn't make out if he was angry with him for stopping Ashtez working or not. He knew her work was very important, but surely the Spirit Master was as excited as he was that they'd found all the families and things that were hiding in the tunnels? Zut had been extremely pleased with him and he was sure that when Ashtez came back that it would be to much more luxurious quarters than they presently had.

Sirleen thanked Epsone for his help, but said that Ashtez could celebrate later as they were very busy at present. Epsone's face disappeared and once again, to Ashtez's relief, the angel's face was back on the screen.

Sirleen tried to smile at Ashtez, but he felt really sick. He didn't tell her that he'd just witnessed all the adults and children being tortured before they were put in the living tubes. Those that survived, of course!

Zut had been so angry when some of the adults hadn't been repaired by the laser program. Sirleen had once again seen them smile as they died and their spirit was taken away by the angels. He had left Zut fuming that the programmer had got in to the laser programs again.

It had slightly worried Sirleen that he hadn't been summoned immediately to the laser room when all the Faith Believers had been captured. Normally as soon as Zut had prisoners, he was the next person Captain Braze contacted. He hoped that Zut wasn't on to him. He wouldn't put it past him to make him watch the Faith Believers being tortured first and then capture him later. Perhaps he needed to put his plan into action now. He wasn't sure if Ashtez was ready, so he thought he'd test her out first.

"So what's your opinion on this program? Do you think it's the truth? Is our leader wrong to put your parents in the living tubes?"

He prayed she would answer correctly. He watched and waited, but Ashtez was unable to speak. Behind Sirleen was an angel! A real, live angel! She could barely believe it, but she could almost feel his wings even though he was behind Sirleen.

"What do you think then, Ashtez, are we real and does God exist?" said the beautiful angel, smiling and sending out all his love to her.

"Oh yes, yes, yes!" she said. It was almost a whisper rather than a shout, but Sirleen understood. He knew she was mesmerized by something and thought it was the program until he, too, felt the angel's warmth coming through his back and spreading all around his body. He realized she was staring, but not at him, so turned to look at what it was.

"Archangel Michael. Thank you, thank you for helping us," he gasped in surprise.

He hadn't realized that Archangel Michael had come back with them. He thought he'd left when they entered the teleport, knowing they were now safe.

"Does this mean that Zut knows I am a Faith Believer now?" he asked nervously.

"A Faith Believer!" said Ashtez in surprise. "Does that mean you believe that God exists?"

Sirleen looked at Ashtez. He hoped he hadn't ruined everything now, but he had been taken by surprise when he had seen Archangel Michael behind him. With being summoned so late to the Laser Room, he felt it was because he still needed the angel's support.

He wasn't entirely certain if Ashtez had really meant she believed now and was unsure whether to answer. There was no way that he could deny God's existence now. That would make God angry, or perhaps sad. Either way, Sirleen knew he wouldn't like it.

Ashtez's smile widened. "You believe God exists as well, don't you? I must help you. That's what the angel is asking me to do, isn't he?" she said as she realized what was happening and what the angel had meant.

Sirleen breathed a deep sigh of relief and relaxed. Thank goodness all Zut's subliminal programming had been broken and the angel's messages had got through to her. He turned to thank Archangel Michael, but to his disappointment he had disappeared.

"Yes, Ashtez, the angel wants you to help not just me, but all those people trapped in the living tubes. First, though, there's a very special person that I would like you to meet."

As he led her toward Anjoy's hiding place he started explaining how Zut subliminally controlled everyone, but he had managed to break it by blocking their ears at night.

Ashtez didn't know who she was going to meet, but she felt pretty good at this moment. Up to now she had been a little scared. She had suddenly realized the programs she had been watching were telling the truth and that God did exist, but she had been worried Sirleen would find out. To be told that he was a Faith Believer was a great relief. She would help in any way he wanted her to.

Chapter 27

Between Planet Placillon and Planet Tirleen, Exact Position Uncertain

Vonick felt quite proud of himself as he looked at all the monitors. He was flying this giant spaceship! It was totally different to his small laser jet that was quite minute compared to this ship, and yet somehow with all of the others helping they had managed to take off and were now flying deep in space. He hadn't a clue where, mind you! Doug and Garm were still trying to work out the program that showed how to control their destination. At least they were off that awful planet. He wasn't in the least worried at what fate beheld the Tirleens that would now be stranded there. They could look after themselves! He, on the other hand, had a far more important mission to do. God's children still needed rescuing!

"We did it, everyone, we are safe and far away from Placillon thanks to you all helping," he said.

"How do you know it wasn't my prayers that did it?" said Cordelius.

"Ah!" said Vonick, unsure what to answer, because he couldn't be sure that it wasn't God who had helped them! "Well, whatever, or whoever helped, we are free. Now all we have to do is find out how to get to Tirleen."

Doug looked at the different programs, trying to work out what they all meant. If only Vonick realized how dangerous Tirleen was going to be then he wouldn't be in such a hurry to reach it. He had been terrified when he realized the porthole had taken them to the wrong planet and even more so when they were captured by the Placillions. Mind torture was a powerful thing. Still, it was their minds that had enabled them to escape and as for finding this spaceship, well, that was out of this world! *Which was where they were at this moment,* he thought and unless he worked out this program, that was where they would stay!

"I don't suppose there's an angel that can understand computer programs, is there?" laughed Doug.

"Actually, there is an angel for everything. I do know that Archangel Uriel is the angel of all systems and sciences, so perhaps we could call upon him and ask him for his help," said Cordelius, laughing at Doug's surprise.

"Do it, please," asked Vonick. "We need as much help as we can. Even divine intervention!"

Cordelius sat quietly and allowed his mind to relax. He asked Archangel Uriel to come into the spaceship and stand close to Doug and Garm and give them some help to work out the program that would enable them to find Planet Tirleen.

He watched Doug and Garm as they frantically pressed more buttons on the program and patiently waited. Less buttons suddenly seemed to be getting pressed and the tension was disappearing from Doug and Garm's faces as they seemed to realize what they were doing at last. Doug pointed to something on the screen and Garm nodded.

Cordelius thanked Archangel Uriel. He knew they had received his help and would soon be on Planet Tirleen. He prayed that Archangel Michael would be waiting for them, because he felt sure they would need a warrior who would fight and protect them and be close by their side at all times.

"It's done, Captain. We are heading toward Tirleen," said Garm excitedly.

"You do know how to land this ship, don't you?" said Doug, who was now a little fretful as he wondered how they would get down. They had managed to get it up, but would they now be doomed to continually fly around space?

"I'm sure we'll manage," said Vonick, hoping he sounded confident and wondering if there was an angel that flew spaceships he could pray to!

The sky suddenly became jet black and they couldn't see where they were flying.

"What's this?" said Vonick, now panicking. What were they heading toward now?

Chapter 28

Planet Tirleen
The Search Begins

Cordelius looked at the screen. He knew what it was! He had flown flew this sort of atmosphere before on his astral travels.

"It's the dark angels. We must be on Tirleen," he said, looking at Doug and Garm for confirmation.

They checked the program and confirmed to Vonick that Cordelius was right. Vonick didn't want to admit he was scared, but this was something he had never experienced before. Darkness! The ship was now rocking from side to side as if the energy was pulling it down.

"They will have lowered the energy on the planet. We will have to be very careful when we land. People will be feeling depressed, angry and even destructive. It may be that nobody will help us and we will have to find the angel children on our own," said Cordelius, totally forgetting everything that he taught his followers and that God was with them all the time.

He had been told by the angels that he had to raise the energy on this planet, but how was he going to do it? It was darker and the energy was lower than he was expecting.

Everyone jumped into their seats and buckled themselves up as the ship suddenly lurched violently from side to side. Doug's head was spinning and he felt quite sick. He was sure they were going to crash and all be killed. No one would be rescued then!

Vonick desperately tried to take control of the ship. He only had a vague notion of what he should do and wasn't sure he knew how to land it. He found himself praying aloud.

"If there is a spaceship angel, then please help me land this ship. I beg of you."

Cordelius heard Vonick praying. Like Doug, he felt dizzy and sick but was desperately praying for the same angel to help them land and added to his prayer, "plus any angel that wants to help."

There was a loud *bang* and a violent bump as the ship crashed to the ground. Some of the lights went off, but a few remained on so they were able to see each other. They all felt their bodies and to their relief nothing was missing or broken. Quickly they unbuckled themselves. They knew the crash must have made a lot of noise. Everyone would know that they were there. *Their plans to creep in and land unseen hadn't worked,* thought Doug!

Vonick stood at the exit door, his laser pin ready to fire. He wasn't sure if it would be of any protection against the people on this planet. Doug had told him he had seen the plans for the weapons the Searchers took with them on their missions, but he didn't know if anyone else used them. He described the "searching wire" that they used. They fired it anywhere at the victim and it immediately searched until it found the spinal cord and severed it from the neck downward, instantly paralyzing them.

The Planet Force guards, on the other hand, just used brute force because no one every argued with them due to their subliminal programming. When the Planet Force guards ordered you to do something, you did it without questioning. Vonick prayed that if they had a welcome, or rather unwelcome, committee waiting for them, that it was the Planet Force guards because their laser pins would soon sort them out!

Silently he said a quick prayer asking Archangel Michael to help them. Cordelius had told him he was the fighter. *Thank goodness at least one of the angels was a fighter,* he thought as he prayed to him. He understood that type of angel.

The doors opened and to their relief there was no one around. Doug trembled as he took his first step back on Tirleen soil after twelve years. It still looked the same, although with the dark angels covering the planet it now felt worse. The depression hit him straight away and he wanted to run away and hide.

Cordelius felt the same but a voice in his head kept saying, "lift the energy." *How did one do it on a place like this?* he thought.

"Cordelius, those words you taught us on Placillon to get us through the rock, would it help to make us feel happier now?" whispered Garm. He didn't want the captain to know how scared he was.

Cordelius realized his prayers had been answered. All they had to do was keep repeating the word "Om" to themselves. It would raise their energy and make them feel stronger and less scared.

Doug looked around Tirleen as he kept repeating "Om" over and over again. He knew where they were. He couldn't believe their luck. They were by the Animal Cloning Market, right near where the porthole had been when they'd left. He prayed it was still there and hadn't moved.

Vonick and the others followed him as he carefully felt for the different energy in the atmosphere. He only wanted to feel it, not fall through it; not yet, anyhow! As he got near the rock and the same spot they'd left through twelve years ago, he felt a tingling in his fingers. Suddenly his hand disappeared and he felt himself falling. Vonick quickly grabbed him and pulled him back.

"It's still in the same spot," he said, smiling with relief.

"Good," said Vonick. "I just hope it's still goes back to the same place!" He didn't want to find themselves on another planet, especially if it was Placillon!

Doug took them into the tunnels and told them they were safe in there as no one ever used the tunnels. Now they could make plans as to what they should do next.

"I thought you said the angel children were hiding in the tunnels?" whispered Vonick after they'd been walking for what seemed miles and miles and still hadn't found any of the children or their families.

"Somewhere," said Doug, "but these tunnels go all around the planet." Doug prayed they weren't lost. They were now all very tired and absolutely starving. They'd found a few rations of food on the spaceship, but he'd forgotten how strange and plain Tirleen food was. He'd gotten used to eating well on Trehf.

"What's that light?" whispered Cordelius as a light appeared ahead of them.

"It could be the angel children; they may have some laser lights on. Quietly walk toward it since we don't want to scare them. They may think we are the Planet Force guards," whispered Doug, hoping they had found the children and could get off Tirleen as quickly as possible.

Cordelius silently prayed to Archangel Michael to be with them and protect them as they slowly and quietly walked toward the light. God was listening as the rest of them did the same. He smiled to himself. If only they realized Archangel Michael had been behind them all the time and it was Archangel Gabriel's light that was guiding them out of the tunnels before they got lost! As the light got brighter, Doug realized they were getting near an exit. He put his hand out to stop the others from going any further.

"It's the way out. We must be very careful we are not seen. It would look very strange if all of us start appearing out of the tunnels. Our clothing is very different from theirs."

Vonick, Garm and the rest of the laser jet crew lined up, ready to lead the way out and protect the other two. Their laser shields would protect them and they also had their laser pins, which had their fingers primed and ready to use at the first sign of trouble. Doug and Cordelius stood well behind, but strangely enough both felt really strong and confident. They didn't realize that Archangel Michael had wrapped his wings around them and had his sword pointed out, ready to protect them!

Vonick slowly peered out of the tunnel and stared in amazement. The buildings were so strange. He looked into a very large one and through the glass he could see it was packed full of people, not unlike Doug in looks, but they all seemed to be drunk! He put his head back in and told Doug what he had seen to see if he had any idea where they were and if it was safe to leave.

"Sounds like the Galiquer if they are all drunk. That's what a bar is called here. It's the only pleasure they have apart from the new Lens and Gaming drome that Zut's built."

"Is it safe to leave, though?" asked Vonick.

"Not really. We are in the most dangerous position of all. Zut's drome, the Planet Force headquarters and the Spirit Master's drome are all near here. None of those people will help us, but we don't want to wander around the tunnels and get lost, so we'll have to risk it."

Cautiously they all left the tunnel and the rest of the group stared at the Galiquer and the other strange buildings.

Chapter 29

Round Three to the Spirit Master

Ashtez looked at more of the programs that Sirleen had been given by the Faith Believers. No wonder Zut was controlling them all, he *must* know that God existed and that was why he put the subliminal messages out at night when they slept. He was scared of God because he was more powerful than him, despite all his great knowledge of how to program and create life, Zut knew that he could never match God's power and once people felt God's love he would no longer be in control of this planet. They would realize how wrong it was to live in such sparse quarters and for all their tirns to end up back with Zut.

"Did you see Odraine and Viola today?" said Sirleen, making Ashtez jump as he teleported into the room.

"Yes, but I didn't dare to stop near their tubes. The Planet Force guards seem to be everywhere."

"Zut still thinks that Zincon is alive and will take over the planet, so he has his guards looking everywhere, especially the living tubes in case he has found a way to free the people in them.

Ashtez continued to read about God and how the world was created. Sirleen smiled as he sat next to her, noticing how calm and happy she looked. It had been wonderful seeing her expression when she'd met Anjoy for the first time and watched as she allowed tears to run down her face, seeing her experience the feeling of love and joy as God wrapped his arms around both of them. Anjoy was still hidden, it wasn't safe to let her join them in here yet, Zut could teleport in at any time and find her.

"Do you think Zut knows that God does exist and is scared of him?" Anjoy asked.

"I've often wondered that," Sirleen replied.

Everything was making sense to him now that he was thinking for himself. He had wondered for a while if Zut had always known about God. He had taken over as leader of the planet at twenty-five years of age when Sirleen was only fifteen. He was starting to remember what life was like then and he knew it was very different. There was no cerebrumadrome then, he felt sure they had been taught differently.

The one thing he had remembered was that God was openly spoken about. Not everyone believed in him but you were allowed to speak his name and talk about him openly without fear of imprisonment. Zut must have started his subliminal programming and creating people himself soon after becoming leader.

Sirleen rubbed the top of his head as he recalled the Planet Force guards rounding them up and taking them to the Wiring Room and then after that nothing, it was all a blank. A lot of people seemed to have disappeared, now he realized they had probably died when the wires were implanted in the fourth lobe of their cerebrums.

Zut had obviously taken a risk doing that to the older ones, or perhaps he didn't care, because it was mostly the older people who believed and spoke about God. Which was probably why there were only a few secret Faith Believers left now. He had planned everything so well. Up to now! Now it looked like God was winning this battle.

Sirleen was a little worried however, the dark angels were creating a lot of negative energy on the planet and tensions were running high. More people were arguing and getting very aggressive. He felt sure it wouldn't be long before they all turned against Zut, which would be good, but on the other hand could be bad. They could also turn on him and the angel children. He prayed that the rescuers that the angel had told him about would soon be here and help him free everyone and then take them all away through one of these portholes that he was yet to find.

Sirleen and Ashtez both jumped in fright as Hurlen, his face contorted and red with rage, teleported into the room screaming at Ashtez as he demanded to know why she was spending all her time here and not down at the new Lens and Gaming drome. She trembled as he carried on screaming at her that he hadn't battled against her on any of the new lens games and she had no right being here and leaving him all alone with the awful wizends. It wasn't fair that she was sleeping here in better quarters whilst he was living with them.

Sirleen immediately saw his chance to get more of the children out of Zut's subliminal programming. He waited for Hurlen to finish venting his anger at Ashtez, smiled at him and quickly put his suggestion to him, hoping that he took the bait.

"Why don't you stay here, too, Hurlen?"

Hurlen's face immediately relaxed. He couldn't believe it, the Spirit Master was inviting him to stay here too! He readily accepted and then demanded that Ashtez leave with him for the Lens and Gaming drome right away. Ashtez realized what Sirleen was up to and quickly stopped Hurlen from teleporting out. She showed him what she was working on to help the Spirit Master. As Hurlen watched the program on angels his body visibly relaxed and he smiled at Ashtez.

"She's beautiful, isn't she?"

Ashtez nodded at him, then looked at Sirleen. She didn't know what to do next. She knew she would only be able to keep him transfixed for so long whilst he was still being subliminally programmed.

Hurlen listened with wide eyes as Sirleen increased the bait and told him how Zut updated all the lens programs at night and if he was in the Lens and Gaming drome on the 1,000th wixon he would see it happen and find out the secret traps that Zut put in to catch them. He could tell all the other children this as well, in confidence, of course, but they had to make sure their ears were blocked. That was vitally important, as whilst Zut was reprogramming the games a lot of whiny noises could be heard and that would distract them.

Hurlen was overjoyed to be given this information and from the Spirit Master no less. He couldn't wait to find the other children and tell them. They were all starting to get angry that the Lens and Gaming drome closed at night and they were ordered to return to their quarters. Now, though, not only had he'd been given this information, but the Spirit Master had also told him how to get into the Lens and Gaming drome at night. Besides, the Spirit Master had said, surely they had a right to play there when they wanted to?

Hurlen didn't wait for Ashtez and immediately teleported out, his face beaming. He was in a rush to impart this secret information to all his friends. The Spirit Master was right; how dare their leader ban them from the Lens Room at night. It was their favourite drome!

Ashtez looked at Sirleen. She was really impressed. Now they would have all the children helping too. Time was running out to help God's miracles and their families to escape. Even she knew that. The dark angels had almost completely covered their planet.

The room suddenly shone with light and they both had to shield their eyes until they could adjust them to it. Ashtez was transfixed. In front of Sirleen and herself were four angels. Not one, but four! It was the most beautiful sight she had ever seen. She wanted to touch their feathers and see if they were as soft as they looked.

Archangel Gabriel spoke first. The other three were Michael, Uriel and Rafael, all Archangels sent by God to give Sirleen a message and make him realize how important it was. Archangel Michael carried a sword and looked very impressive. He was a fighting angel. Ashtez had been surprised when Sirleen had told her this after his last visit, as she didn't know that angels fought.

She barely heard a word that Gabriel said as she stared at them. Michael noticed and walked toward her. At first she was a little afraid, but when he touched her hand she instantly felt his love pouring through her body. He let her stroke his feathers and touch his face.

Sirleen listened to Gabriel's message. It appeared that the rescuers were here on Tirleen, but they were in great danger. They were all walking toward the Planet Force guards and if they were caught would not be able to free anyone. He was to teleport straight to the Galiquer and stop them from wandering any further, then bring them back to his quarters. Sirleen left Ashtez still in a daze and also slightly disappointed when the four angels disappeared with him.

Chapter 30

ASHTEZ SOLVES THE PROBLEM

Doug screamed as Sirleen appeared in front of them. He was so scared that he didn't notice the four angels surrounding Sirleen. Cordelius wondered what was wrong with Doug since he could see the angels, especially Michael, who had his sword out ready to protect them. He hadn't noticed that in the middle of the angels was a man.

"It's the Spirit Master, run!" Doug yelled, turning to run back into the tunnels. The others immediately followed. Doug had told them all about the Spirit Master, whose task it was to tell people why God was a fairy tale. They definitely didn't want to tangle with him!

The four angels left Sirleen and blocked the entrance to the tunnel. Doug and the others were terrified and wondered what the angels were doing. Why were they letting the Spirit Master capture them?

"Stop!" yelled Sirleen. "Please don't be afraid of me. I no longer believe what Zut has programmed everyone else to believe. I am now a Faith Believer."

Doug stared at Sirleen in total disbelief. Did the Spirit Master just say he was a Faith Believer? Surely not? It must be a trick. Hadn't the angels realized this man's task was to make people believe they didn't exist?

"Yes, I know it is hard for you to believe, especially you, Doug, but I found out about the subliminal program and now that I can think for myself I realize Zut was wrong. God does exist and I must help you to free all of his angel children."

Doug wondered how he knew about him. He had not lived here for over twelve years. Did that mean that Zut was still looking for them? Was his family safe back on Trehf?

"Don't look so scared, Doug," said Sirleen, noticing his worried face. "Archangel Gabriel has told me how you used to live here and were coming back to help with the rescue. Remember Zut used to program me so that when you escaped no one remembered that you and your family ever existed."

Doug relaxed. Thank goodness Cedra and his children were safe.

Sirleen checked if it was safe to enter the teleport and then took them all back to his drome. The angels stayed with them all the time until they were sure they were safe.

They joined Anjoy and all of them felt the great joy she gave out as God filled her with love and sent it out to them. *She was aptly named,* thought Doug. Now they realized they were right in coming on this mission and were all glad that they hadn't ignored the angel's message. Even though it had been terrifying on Placillon, they had to rescue the rest of God's miracles no matter what challenges were thrown at them from now on.

Sirleen left them and rejoined Ashtez. Now that she believed God existed he had to get her some help to free everyone in the living tubes. Ashtez looked at the program for the living tubes. She didn't know how Sirleen had managed to steal these from Zut. He had taken a great risk, but then so was she now that she was a Faith Believer. That was dangerous in itself, but somehow she had to break this program and free all the other believers trapped in the living tubes. If ever Zut found out she had done it, she would never be a Searcher. She suddenly realized that didn't matter any longer. Now she wanted to be free with Anjoy and her family and away from Planet Tirleen.

Sirleen said the rescuers had arrived and were safely hidden with Anjoy. She prayed Zut didn't find them because they were going to help her and everyone else leave this planet.

She was amazed at how clever Zut's program was for the living tubes. He had used all the properties of a placenta, something his notes said babies used to breathe before they were born. They were surrounded by amniotic fluid and this along with the information fed through the wires attached to the program kept them alive. She had noticed the long tube attached to their abdomens and had often wondered what it was and how it kept them alive. All the tubes were connected to a program in the wiring room.

If she could change the wiring program that would free them all. Or would it kill them all? Ashtez realized she had a problem, Zut had been extremely clever. The wiring program was controlling their brain to tell then to breathe using the amniotic fluid, but if she changed it and they weren't still connected to the tube inside, would they die? Did she have to do something with the tube as well?

She discussed the situation with Sirleen. This not only made sense to him but seemed to be triggering something in his brain, something from the past. What was it? He just couldn't recall it at the moment. He decided to try and find some old files from the year 2010, way before he was born. The word "born" seemed to trigger something. That was it! He hadn't been created by Zut. Although Zut's father, Zirk, who was leader then, was also very ruthless. Perhaps he had been created by him? It was all very confusing, yet somehow he knew that people were created differently in the past.

"I'm going to Zut's quarters to see if I can find some old files that may help."

Ashtez immediately panicked. If Sirleen was caught stealing any files she would be left alone to continue the fight, unless of course they searched his quarters and arrested her, too!

Sirleen left her puzzling over the program and teleported into the underbase of Zut's quarters and walked straight into Zut. He tried not to show any panic on his face and started thinking quickly of an excuse as to why he was there. Should he risk exposing Ashtez and telling Zut she was trying to help break the things' programs, or if Zut suspected her, would that then put her in danger too?

"What are you doing in this area?" demanded Zut.

"I thought I'd see if there was some really old data on God and angels that I could use to convince the people that Zincon is wrong and that you, our great leader, has always been right. Tensions are running high all over the planet. I hoped that if I could find something really powerful to use against Zincon's so-called "things" that it would help," he said, trying not to stammer.

Zut looked at Sirleen suspiciously, trying to decide if he was telling the truth or not. He had been acting very oddly recently, even questioning him about some of his decisions. He decided to trust him because at this moment everyone seemed to be questioning his abilities as leader. He, too, was in the underbase looking for some old data to see if he could use it to bring the light back into his planet. That would certainly make people realize how clever he was.

"Carry on then. Take what you need. We must do something and quickly. If only I could find Zincon again and the one remaining "thing" of his and get them in a living tube, then that would show everyone that I am still in control," he said angrily as he teleported out with something in his hand.

Sirleen wondered what Zut had found. Whatever it was he knew that he couldn't create any program to bring light back in, only God could get rid of the dark angels and bring back the light. Quickly he searched for something to help them. He didn't want to leave Ashtez alone for too long. He didn't trust Zut; he may well have bluffed his way around Zut this time, but even now he could be changing his mind about him. The dark energy was changing everyone's personalities, including Zut's. He was becoming more and more ruthless in his anger and desperation to be recognized as the leader. If only he knew that right now Zincon was probably looking down from Heaven, laughing at him and not hiding on the planet anywhere!

Ashtez breathed a sigh of relief when Sirleen rejoined her. She was starting to get scared and had thought of joining Anjoy and the others and hiding with them. She didn't know if Sirleen had been arrested or not, or if Zut knew she was here helping Sirleen in his quest to free God's gifts.

She felt quite proud as she showed Sirleen how she could change the program in the Wiring Room, but that would mean either going into the room to do it, or using Zut's quarters. She felt the Wiring Room would be the safer option, as she may be able to convince the operators that Zut had sent her. They all knew she was the Wiron Leader, so she would use that title to her advantage and hope they didn't question her too much. Before she changed any programs, though, she had to be sure she wouldn't kill everyone in the living tubes when she did it.

They both studied the files that Sirleen had taken. As she watched the creation of life from the past, Ashtez realized how Zut had used this information to enable people to remain in the living tubes until they were two hundred and fifty years old.

"This is very clever, isn't it?" said Sirleen. "But you do realize that in the past life only lived for so long in that fluid, so how has Zut managed to make these people live longer?"

Ashtez pondered over the question. Sirleen realized the answer before she did. The subliminal program! Of course, they wouldn't know if any of them died in the tubes or not. Zut would just reprogram everyone to forget and change the population numbers. That didn't help Ashtez much, though, it just made her realize how dangerous it would be when she changed the wiring data. How did they get all the people out of the tubes and make sure they were still alive?

"We will need a lot of help to get the people free. There are so many of them in living tubes now," she said.

"Yes, about two hundred and fifty. I had forgotten how many there were as they are scattered all around the planet," said Sirleen, remembering how many he had passed on his walk that day.

"If only we could find a way to use Zut's subliminal program to our advantage," Ashtez sighed.

Sirleen looked at Ashtez in surprise. She really was clever; no wonder she had found and beaten the hidden robot lens. She could match Zut's brain any time. This was the answer. If they could tell everyone to help them free the people, then it would be so easy to escape. Ashtez could probably easily change the subliminal program, but what did they do about Zut? Was he awake when the program came on at the 1,000th wixon, or did he have it set up ready to come on then?

Sirleen decided that Zut wouldn't risk it not working and probably would be still awake when it came on. What they needed was some way to either knock Zut out whilst they did the reprogramming, or lock him up and make him forget who he was.

They both suddenly realized that Zut was the only person not to have wires coming out of his fourth lobe. What did that mean? How did he get repaired if anything happened? Would he live until he was two hundred and fifty years of age?

Chapter 31
HURLEN BELIEVES

Hurlen yawned for probably the hundredth time. He was exhausted but at the same time exhilarated. Last night had been fantastic. He'd found out how to get through several of the traps set by Zut. At this rate, with all his extra wiring practice, he'd take Ashtez's title off her and be the new Wiron Leader next Given. His head was still buzzing when he took the game lenses off. He could barely see his friends where his eyes were so bleary.

The was the second night he'd been in the Lens and Gaming drome along with the rest of the children. They couldn't believe their luck when Hurlen told them not only how to get into the drome, but that Zut put all the new traps in at the 1,000th wixon. They had all sneaked in after they were ordered to leave, but kept a close eye on the wixons. At precisely the 1,000th wixon they all blocked their ears and watched the screens. Surprisingly enough nothing seemed to happen on the screens, but somehow by the second night, even if their gaming skills hadn't improved, they all felt confident that they would eventually beat Zut.

The children checked that no one was around and trooped out in small groups to catch the flier to cerebrumadrome. Hurlen yawned again. He was so tired. He wondered if he could sneak back to the Spirit Master's quarter and catch up on his sleep in that wonderfully soft and luxurious bed. Lorn, who was accompanying him, looked shattered, too, and they both yawned in unison.

They decided to give cerebrumadrome a miss, so were walking home, having reached the decision that too many questions may be asked on the flier. They weren't going to let Zut order them to do something they didn't want to do and as well as not going to cerebrumadrome today, if they didn't feel like it tomorrow, then they wouldn't go then either! They stopped and stared into the living tubes at their parents. Lorn looked at Brade, next to his mother.

"Mum says he's my brother, sent from God," he said as he placed his hand on the glass to match Brade's. Lorn's eyes filled with tears as he felt his brother's love and pain.

"Help us, please," said a voice in his head.

Lorn stared into the tube. How could he be hearing Brade's voice if he was in there, and was he really his brother? He turned to ask Hurlen what he thought, but Hurlen was hugging the tube with his mother in and sobbing his eyes out.

"Mum, I miss you so, so much."

Lorn gently pulled him away and they fell into each others arms and cried copiously.

"I hate Zut. I'm going to get him for what he did to my parents," yelled Hurlen.

He was spitting with anger. How dare that man put his parents in one of these things! Lorn agreed. They decided to get some sleep first, then they would decide how to free their parents and get their revenge.

Hurlen left Lorn at his drome and carried on walking to the Spirit Master's quarters. The more living tubes he passed the angrier he became. He didn't know if this God existed or not but that picture Ashtez showed him of the angel was really beautiful and just thinking about it made him feel warm and happy.

He crept into his sleeping quarter and snuggled into the soft bed. His eyes flickered as he fell into a deep sleep. He floated around with the angels and laughed as their feathers tickled him. He felt safe and loved, and he listened as they told him to help free everyone from the living tubes and save all of God's gifts.

He woke up with tears in his eyes, feeling happy, yet sad that the angels were no longer with him. He remembered all they had said and thought about Anjoy. Was she really his sister and if so, where was she now? All the parents and the rest of the angel children were in the living tubes, but Anjoy wasn't there.

He wondered if he could risk asking Ashtez about her or if she'd get really annoyed, especially as they were living in the Spirit Master's quarters now. He didn't want him thinking he was a...his thoughts stopped. If he believed in the angels, did that make him a Faith Believer? He felt sure that the beautiful angels did exist. He didn't know why he felt that because he'd never heard or seen an angel before coming to the Spirit Master's quarters, but now, now he'd flown with them!

He whistled as he went to join Ashtez, still trying to decide whether to ask her about Anjoy. Ashtez was rewriting the final stage of the wiring program to free everyone. It was almost ready to use. She just had to work out how to get them out of the tubes now. She smiled as Hurlen sat next to her. He was obviously experiencing what it felt like to be alive and not have his brain subliminally programmed by Zut. She hoped it was having the same effect on the other children too. She quickly changed the screen so that an angel's face appeared and watched Hurlen as he stared and smiled at the angel.

"I saw Mum and Dad in the living tubes today," he said cautiously, watching for her reaction.

Ashtez wondered if the time was right to say how she felt, then seeing how sad Hurlen looked when he mentioned their parents, she decided to go for it. She told him she had visited them several times because she missed them so much and she didn't think they should be in there.

Hurlen gasped with surprise and relief that his sister had the same thoughts as he did.

"Do you think Anjoy is our sister then?"

"Yes, she is our sister and a gift from God."

Hurlen smiled, relieved that Ashtez felt the same as him, but at the same time sad because if Anjoy was their sister, then where was she?

"Have you seen a real angel, sis?" he asked.

Ashtez's face lit up as she remembered the four Archangels and Michael as he allowed her to stroke his face and feathers. "Oh yes! They are beautiful and soft and full of love." She hugged Hurlen as she saw the relief on his face that it was OK to talk about angels and believe that they existed.

"Does this mean we are Faith Believers now?" he nervously asked.

"Yes, indeed you are!" boomed Sirleen's voice.

Hurlen screamed and trembled as Sirleen stood in front of them. The Spirit Master had caught them saying they were Faith Believers! Now they would end up in a living tube next to their parents. He grabbed Ashtez's hand, intending to flee, but Sirleen placed a firm hand on his shoulder and, to his surprise, hugged him, then looked at him with a big smile on his face.

"And so, Hurlen, am I!"

Wow! Hurlen took a step backward and stared as Ashtez nodded, a big smile on her face. Sirleen sat him down and gently explained about Zut's subliminal program that was why no one believed in God, but by blocking their ears on the 1,000th wixon they were able to start thinking for themselves. God had really sent twenty-five gifts to the planet and it was his and Ashtez's task to help save them.

"Our sister Anjoy, she's dead isn't she? She's not with the other children, so she must have died."

He sobbed in Ashtez's arms, so upset that God had sent his sister back to them and that he'd never met her because he didn't believe in her. He barely heard Ashtez as she told him Anjoy was still alive, so she repeated it again. He looked up and in a daze allowed them to lead him to where Anjoy was hidden.

Anjoy hugged and kissed her brother and he sobbed again, only this time with joy as he told her how much he loved her.

Hurlen suddenly became aware of more people in the room. All were in very strange clothing and some of them had some sort of weapon in their hands. He was ecstatic when they said they had been sent to rescue God's angel children and the Faith Believers. Here was someone who would help him free his parents.

He sat and listened with sheer admiration for his sister as Ashtez explained how she had changed the wiring program, but she would need help getting everyone out of the living tubes by cutting and tying those cords before they could be released. It also had to be done quickly because as soon as she changed the wiring program, unless they were freed from the fluid quickly, then they would drown.

"The children will help, I know they will," said Hurlen, anxious to help.

Sirleen smiled, thinking of Zut's anger if he ever found out that by building the Lens and Gaming drome it had led the way to his subliminal programming being broken by all the children. Now they would get all the help they needed because the living tubes were scattered all around the planet and there were many of them. They were just left with the problem of how to change the program so that everyone felt the same. They also wondered what to do with Zut whilst they were doing it.

Chapter 32
ZUT TAKES THE BAIT

Zut frowned as Sirleen's face appeared on the screen. He was just on his way to his sleeping quarters to check that the subliminal program came on. Even though it was set to start at the exact time every night, he still liked to make sure it happened. He didn't want any slip-ups; just one night without the subliminal program and his people would start thinking for themselves and would soon realize how much he controlled them. He was also annoyed that Sirleen was still awake.

His frown changed to a big grin, and he jumped up and down with joy as Sirleen imparted his news. Instead of going to his sleeping quarters, he teleported to the Evaporation Room since that was the nearest port to the tunnels. The subliminal program would be fine. It was set so nothing could possibly go wrong with it but the news Sirleen had just given him couldn't wait.

Telepathically he ordered all of the Planet Force guards to meet him at the same tunnel. He couldn't wait to see Zincon's face when they arrested him again and this time there was no way he'd escape when he was wired up.

Whilst he was ecstatically making his way to the tunnel, Sirleen was showing Ashtez where Zut's sleeping quarters were. Without the guards around they could move freely and without fear of getting caught.

Ashtez quickly changed the program and at exactly the 1,000th wixon the new subliminal message started. She smiled as she listened to Sirleen's voice telling everyone not to listen to their leader, that he was trying to control them for his own means and that he, the Spirit Master, now realized and believed that God existed and that God wanted everyone to help rescue his angel children and the rest of the Faith Believers.

"That's enough for tonight," said Sirleen as Ashtez quickly put Zut's program back in.

"It's a pity the Planet Force guards didn't receive this message as well, though. It would be better if we had them on our side," she said as they hurried to the teleport.

Hurlen and Anjoy breathed a sigh of relief when Sirleen and Ashtez safely returned. They'd been terrified that Zut would return and catch them in his quarters. Now everyone waited for Zut to summon Sirleen once he realized Zincon wasn't there.

Sirleen had made contingency plans in case Zut didn't believe his excuse and arrested him. Everyone had to stay hidden until the next night, then Vonick would go with Ashtez to put the message in and stun Zut with his laser pin. That would give her enough time to play the next part of the message, telling everyone how to help when she changed the wiring program. In the event of Sirleen being placed in a living tube, then they were to carry on without him. Ashtez stayed with the rest of the group and once more went over their plans whilst Sirleen hurried back to wait for his call.

Sirleen hoped his prayers for help and guidance had been heard when Zut summoned him. *This was it,* he thought as he made his way to the teleport. If Zut didn't believe him, would he be as brave as Zincon and the others when they were tortured? How horrendous was it to live in one of those tubes? He tried to remain calm as he entered Zut's quarters and walked in confidently and with a big smile on his face.

"Did you get him?" he said, trying to sound really excited.

"No, he wasn't there!" said Zut angrily, giving Sirleen a suspicious look.

Sirleen looked disappointed and hoped he had fooled Zut. When Zut demanded to know where the information had come from, he quickly explained that Jayfer had been leaving the Galiquer and had seen Zincon enter the tunnels. He'd hurried back to the Galiquer to tell him. He was going to be as disappointed as they were, apart from the fact that the leader of the Faith Believers had escaped again. He knew Jayfer was expecting a big reward from Zut for the information.

Sirleen smiled with relief as he followed Zut to the Wiring Room. He watched and listened with no emotion as Jayfer screamed and denied that he knew where Zincon was and at the same time thanked God that it wasn't him wired up!

Zut's anger increased as Jayfer refused to reveal where Zincon really was and why he'd tricked him. He ordered the power to be increased and smiled as Jayfer yelled as he caught fire then, after being lasered, was put back for another session. He still continued to deny everything.

"This is getting boring," he yelled to Captain Braze. "Put him in the living tube. Let everyone see I am not to be messed with."

Jayfer was unwired and taken out, struggling and screaming, to the tubes. Sirleen watched, still showing no emotion as Jayfer was led out. He hoped he suffered as much pain and fear as he had put his young son, Broocen, through.

He hurried back to his quarters to let everyone know he was safe and had fooled Zut for the moment, at least! He was relieved and surprised to find the four Archangels with them. Michael explained that God had wanted to make sure they were safe in case Zut imprisoned him and then came searching his quarters and found them.

"The next part of your mission will be very dangerous and you must be on your guard at all times. All is not what it seems," said Michael before he disappeared with the other angels.

They looked at each other in fear, wondering what was to befall them now and wishing the angels had stayed so that they could ask Michael what he had meant.

Chapter 33
ZUT HAS AN ACCIDENT

Vonick wiped the perspiration off his forehead as he followed Sirleen and Ashtez to Zut's sleeping quarters to change the program again. He knew he was more protected than they were with his laser pin, which at the moment his finger was nervously touching, ready to fire. If the Planet Force guards appeared, then he'd be one man against many. Who would win the battle?

Cordelius has assured him that although they wouldn't see him, Michael would be with them at all times, protecting them. He prayed it was true, but right now he was shaking with fear. This was one of the scariest missions he'd been sent on. Up to now all the fighting he had experienced had been on his planet and he always had the whole laser jet crew behind him as they fought. Now he was entirely on his own, except for Michael, of course! He prayed for his help as they entered the room.

Zut looked up in surprise as they entered. "What are …?" He got no further as Vonick quickly fired the laser pin, hitting Zut right in the chest. Zut screamed and held his chest as he fell to the floor. Sirleen pushed Ashtez toward the computer as she stared in shock at Zut on the floor.

"Is he dead?" she asked, not realizing that would help their mission.

"No, no, he'll be fine," said Vonick. "This pin just stuns them, but you have to be quick before he comes to."

Ashtez quickly changed the program. Sirleen had to guide her hands as they were shaking so much. Just seeing Zut had unnerved her and even though he was not conscious, she was terrified he would come to and telepathically call the Planet Force guards to arrest them. She could barely concentrate on what she was doing as she imagined what it would be like to be tortured and placed in a tube.

"Concentrate, Ashtez, you are quite safe. We are all here with you," said a voice that seemed to be coming from inside her head. She looked around the room to see if Sirleen had heard it too, but he was still helping her hands change the program.

"Ashtez, it's me, God. Listen to me. Concentrate to help my angel children, please."

"God! Are you really talking to me?" she replied in her head.

"I always talk to you, Ashtez, you just haven't either listened or trusted in yourself that you were really hearing me. Now please relax and concentrate. You are quite safe."

Sirleen watched Ashtez as she smiled and became calm, he wondered if one of the angels was comforting her because she was totally in control now and had the program up and running.

They all listened to the new program and hoped that after tonight everyone would help Ashtez when she changed the wiring program. She quickly put Zut's program in as her nerves returned. She wanted to get out now before Zut surfaced.

"How long before he comes to?" asked Sirleen, who was amazed at how effective the laser pin was.

Vonick looked puzzled as he knelt down to examine Zut. They were normally conscious by now. In fact, he was expecting to have to zap him again before they left. He listened to his chest then looked up and shook his head. Sirleen didn't know whether to feel exhilarated or scared as they realized that Zut was in fact dead and notjust stunned! Ashtez trembled and prayed that none of the guards entered and caught them with Zut's body.

Sirleen grabbed her and pushed her out toward the teleport.

"Come on, let's get out before they find him."

In a trance, she allowed him to lead her to the teleport.

The sweat was dripping off them and they were all trembling as they returned to Sirleen's quarters. Cordelius panicked as they entered; something had obviously gone wrong tonight, but what? Michael was supposed to be protecting them, so what could possibly have happened?

Whilst Anjoy and Hurlen jumped up and down and danced around the room, screaming with joy when Vonick said that Zut had died when he'd been stunned, Sirleen and the rest of them were now realizing what it really meant for them.

"With Zut dead we can carry on and free everyone without any fear at all," said Sirleen, smiling at last.

Hurlen left for the Lens Room with a huge smile on his face, knowing that his parents would soon be free. He hoped none of the children had left because he had to catch all of them and explain what he wanted them to do.

Their original plan to smash the tubes had soon fallen by the wayside when Sirleen realized they would probably not have anything strong enough on the planet to break the glass. Plus, all the fluid would pour out and if the cords weren't cut and tied quickly enough they would die, as the fluid also helped to keep them alive.

Ashtez had found out how Zut sealed the tubes and with a quick adjustment had altered the program so that she could open the top of the tubes. This now meant the children had to climb up the tube and get inside it to cut and tie the cords, then climb out along with its occupant. It was still a bit risky as they would have to hold their breath whilst they did it. At the same time they had to hope the person they were freeing realized they were trying to help and not harm them.

Ashtez, Sirleen and the laser jet crew made their way to the Wiring Room. They could hear loud cheering as they passed the Lens and Gaming drome; the children were obviously delighted that Zut was dead and they would be helping to free everyone. At least they didn't have to worry about the children now. The Planet Force guards having had one night's subliminal program would not ask any questions when they found Zut's body.

They walked into the Wiring Room, anxious to change the program as quickly as possible, but at the same time with no worries about having to make an excuse as to why Ashtez was there and who the other strange people were.

Hurlen and the rest of the children were now on the flier and getting impatient at the amount of time it was taking to get to the animal cloning market. It was the only way to get there and today the two wixons' journey seemed to go on for ever. They knew they were all expected as Sirleen had added a bit in the subliminal message for the chief cloner to give every child a hook, rope and knife to help with the rescue.

As soon as the flier stopped all the children ran into the animal cloning market and grabbed their equipment, then jumped back onto the flier, all getting off at various points around the planet to stand by a living tube, anxious and tense as they waited for it to open.

The occupants of the tubes looked scared as each child stood in front of them and wondered what was going to happen to them now. They were unable to receive the subliminal program inside the tubes, so now realized how many lies had been told, but Zut was not concerned because there was nothing they could say or do now. Those that had been imprisoned for a while had seen their friends die after twelve years in the tubes and not the original two hundred and fifty years as everyone was programmed to think, so they knew their suffering would end, but was this more torture from Zut before they died?

Anjoy was now outside Viola's tube and wishing Hurlen would hurry up with her equipment. She had left him to collect it because she wanted to try and explain to the other angel children what was going to happen in case they thought the children intended to harm them. She wouldn't have time to tell everyone, so they decided she must concentre on her parents and the angel children and pray that the others realized they were being freed.

Broocen felt the warmth and love from her hand as she told him he was going to be freed and they were all going to another planet to live with their parents. She watched in dismay as tears ran down his face and he told her he wanted to go home to God. He didn't like his parents; they were cruel and had put him in the tube and let him be tortured. God was kind and loving and heaven was his home, not with them.

She was trying to explain that Sone and Jayfer had been taken in by Zut and believed his lies and didn't mean to harm him. She was just going to tell him that Jayfer was now also suffering in a tube when Hurlen ran up and handed her some equipment. She quickly smiled at Broocen, gave his tube a hug for him to feel her love, then stood outside her mother's tube with her eyes fixed on the top. She was waiting to spring into action the instant it opened.

Broocen watched in horror as his small sister, Denna, stood outside with her knife in her mouth, hook in hand and rope around her shoulders, ready to climb up and rescue her brother. She desperately wanted to apologize for everything that had happened to him and for them not believing he was real. She hoped her mother had reached the porthole and had some dry clothes for Broocen as the temperature was rapidly dropping on the planet as the dark angels got lower.

God had no control over the dark angels. Once he'd sent his miracles and they were ignored by the planet, the dark angels had descended, ready to embrace all the negative and bad energy they knew would exist when Zut and the rest still refused to believe in God. They fed on negative energy and had tried to fool God by saying they would help in his plan when he sent his gifts to Tirleen. They said by blocking the light and increasing everyone's fear they would make Tirleen realize that God did exist and they should be listening to him and not their leader.

God had known all along that they were working against him, but he hoped that when everyone saw his gifts they would be so overjoyed that they would overpower Zut and their positive energy would kill the dark angels, thus getting rid of them once and for all. But even God isn't perfect! He hadn't realized how powerful the subliminal programming was and so the dark angels' power had increased and he was slowly losing the light from the planet.

His angels were banding together and were at this moment ascending on the planet to help in the fight before the dark angels increased and spread their negative energies and smothered the whole universe. St. Germain was leading the Thrones, Cherubims and Seraphims in their attempt to fight the dark angels, and Archangel Michael would assist when he was sure Ashtez had changed the program and it was safe to leave her. The Guardian and other Archangels were helping to protect the people in their tasks or as they made they way to the porthole, ready to flee.

Chapter 34

ALL IS NOT WHAT IT SEEMS

Ashtez stammered nervously as Mander questioned why she was in the Wiring Room and demanded to know who the strange people were. She didn't know what had gone wrong. Why wasn't he expecting them and helping them? She nearly put them all at risk by mentioning why they were really there, but luckily Sirleen had realized something was wrong. He hastily explained that Ashtez had been sent by Zut to gain more wiring knowledge after her success as Wiron Leader, as it may be that she would be of more use in the Wiring Room than as a Searcher when she joined the Planet Force. He was just trying to think of an excuse as to who the other men were when Vonick came up with the answer.

"We are a secret that only Zut knows about, but he has decided that this is an emergency so we have been sent to look at his wiring program to assist in finding Zincon and the angel children."

Mander smiled and welcomed them all. He was relieved he hadn't made too much of a fuss when they'd rushed into his room. Zut still blamed him for Zincon escaping. This way, if he helped then he may get back into favor with him.

"He particularly wanted Ashtez and the others to see his living tube wiring programs," said Sirleen, smiling at Mander, but still making him aware of how important he was.

Mander led them all to a door marked "no admittance, leader only" and was very disappointed when Sirleen told him they had to look at this on their own. He had never been allowed into this room and was hoping to see what secrets it held, but the Spirit Master was almost as powerful as their leader, so without questioning him any further he pressed the code into the panel, then stared at Sirleen as the door remained closed.

"You have to put Zut's wire in now."

Sirleen tried to remain calm. He didn't want Mander to realize they didn't have Zut's wire and he was still unsure as to why the program hadn't worked last night and why Mander wasn't helping him.

Mander frowned, something didn't feel quite right here. Why hadn't the Spirit Master got Zut's wire? But then why was the Spirit Master trying to break into Zut's room anyhow? He couldn't risk getting into more trouble with Zut. He had already threatened to wire him up if they didn't find Zincon soon.

He hesitated one second too long, as that was when Vonick decided to take control and fired the laser pin at him. Mander screamed as he fell to the floor and then lay unconscious. Ashtez panicked. She hoped he wasn't dead, too; they were supposed to be rescuing people not killing them!

Vonick moved everyone out of the way and fired at the door several times hoping to disable the wire that was preventing it from opening. Nothing seemed to happen, so in his anger and frustration he bashed it with his fist and to his surprise and the others delight, the door swung open and he fell in.

The others quickly followed and closed the door as Vonick got up and tried to regain his dignity. Garm and the rest of his crew tried to stifle their laughter. They looked around the empty room with dismay, wondering what to do next. Where was the wiring program? How could they free people if there was no computer with the data? Sirleen looked closer at the walls as he realized that there were in fact five doors, all of them very cleverly concealed, but once you'd seen one you could recognize the others.

They followed him into the first room and were surprised but disappointed to see it was just a cloning room with rows and rows of tiny living tubes all with a very small fetus inside, some slightly bigger than others. Ashtez realized it was just a smaller version of the tubes her parents were in, so looked around to see if they were programmed from the room somewhere, hoping it would contain the other programs. No one could see anything obvious or hidden anywhere, so they decided to try the next room.

Sirleen held Ashtez tightly as she screamed in horror, whilst he tried to stop himself from doing the same. He could see from the others' faces that it had scared them too. Staring out of bigger living tubes were ten clones of Zut, each one slightly older than the other. The oldest was about fifteen years old. All of the Zuts grinned as the group hastily left the room, trembling and white with shock.

"They can't harm us, Ashtez, they are children and still in the tubes," said Sirleen as he thanked God that no one else knew what was in these rooms apart from Zut, and he was dead. Once they'd found the computer and changed their programs, then he would get Ashtez to destroy all of the Zuts.

Cautiously, Sirleen peered into the next room. Vonick was behind him and ready to fire at anything that attacked him. The relief on Sirleen's face told them it was not only safe to enter, but also the right room. Ashtez ran to the computer and put the new wiring program in. She hastily tapped the keys and hoped that right now all the tubes were opening and the children were climbing in and rescuing the people.

"That's it, they should be free," she yelled as tears of joy ran down her face at the thought of seeing her parents very soon and all of them being free to live on another planet.

"Quickly, find the program for Zut's clones and break them. We must flee as soon as possible before the dark angels take all the air away from the planet. God is not sure how long his angels can hold them back, or if they can fight them all," said Sirleen, anxious to get out of the building and make their way to the porthole.

Ashtez looked through Zut's programs and realized why he had no wires himself in his brain. He had cloned himself so many times and at different stages in his life that there would always be a Zut in control and with his subliminal programming no one would ever know any difference.

"Got it!" she said as she found the main program and went to delete it.

"Leave my babies alone," said a voice from behind.

Ashtez was surprised when she could hear her voice screaming, because the rest of her was paralyzed with fear. Standing behind them was Zut and he had a searching wire in his hand. Before Vonick could react, Garm and the rest of the crew instinctively fired their laser pins at Zut. Their screams echoed around the room as the laser rebounded and the searching wire hit their bodies and quickly located their spinal cords. In seconds they were all led paralyzed and dying on the floor as Zut grinned at the others. Vonick screamed as his voice came back and he stared in horror at his men. He, too, had been paralyzed with fear when Zut had appeared, but for once his fear had saved his life. So far anyway!

"Didn't expect to see me when the last one died, did you?" Zut grinned at them.

Ashtez prayed the rest of the people were still being rescued and the Planet Force guards hadn't stopped them. She didn't know what to do now, but found herself talking to God in her mind.

"Help us, please, God. What can we do? How can we get out now?"

"Just by trusting me," said God.

"Trust?" said Ashtez, wondering how trust was going to get them out of this extremely sticky and dangerous situation.

"Trust," said God.

As Ashtez was puzzling over his answer, Michael, Gabriel, Uriel and Raphael appeared and surrounded Zut. Whilst the others could see Zut and watch as Michael put his sword through his body, all that Zut could seen was a bright light and feel intense pain as he lay on the floor, bleeding and dying.

Sirleen grabbed Ashtez by the hand and the three of them ran out and almost fell over Mander, who was standing guard outside the room. Zut had reprogrammed him again and now he was under strict instructions not to let them leave the building. He held a searching wire in his trembling hand and hoped he didn't have to use it. He wasn't sure if he was brave enough to press the wire, knowing it would harm them.

Vonick recognized the fear in Mander's eyes, but didn't dare risk firing his laser pin, knowing now that it would rebound and harm him. The only advantage they had was that they knew Zut, or one of them, was dead, whilst Mander didn't, and he was trembling as he waited for Zut to appear and take over. Sirleen decided that this was one of those occasions when bravery and brute force were needed.

He hoped he looked convincing when he stared behind Mander with his face contorted in horror. Mander trembled and quickly looked behind to see what was scaring Sirleen. In the split second it took him to take his eyes off them, Sirleen bashed Mander on the top of his head with both of his fists with as much force as he could render.

Vonick watched the pain and shocked look in Mander's eyes as he collapsed to the floor and lay dazed. Quickly and carefully he extracted the searching wire from him, then added insult to injury by stunning him with his laser pin.

They left Mander staring into space as they ran out of the Wiring Room and into total chaos as the people battled with the Planet Force guards as they tried to escape.

Some of the living tubes were already empty and Doug was just pulling an astonished and relieved Rone out his. Rone shivered as he felt the cold air and breathed deeply to get control of his lungs and get his first taste of life as a free man. Doug smiled. His friend was free after all that time imprisoned in the tube and soon he would be back with them on Trehf and able to enjoy life once again.

He turned to lead Rone to the porthole but was abruptly stopped. There was a *crack* as his face connected with Captain Braze's fist, and he fell to the ground, screaming with pain. Captain Braze's grin soon changed to horror as he pulled Doug up off the floor, ready to hit him again. Doug remembered the knife he held and thrust it straight into Captain Braze's chest and watched his grin fade as the blood poured out.

He stared at the blood on his knife, and his knees buckled. He could hear Rone's trembling voice asking if he was OK and realized this was no time for weakness. He had to help Rone to the porthole. After all that time in the tube he would still be a bit weak and they had a long way to go yet. He wiped the blood off the knife and put it in his pocket, hoping he wouldn't have to use it again. He put his arm around Rone and helped him to walk as they followed the others as they fled.

As they passed the empty living tubes, Doug smiled with relief and thanked God for helping the children to free them, but then also adding a quick prayer to help the souls of those unfortunate one who had either drowned, or were strangled by the cord as they'd obviously panicked when the children tried to free them, thinking they were intending to harm them.

Viola watched with tears in her eyes as Hurlen and Anjoy desperately battled to save Broocen and pull him out of the tube. Denna had tried to free him, but he'd struggled and panicked so much when she'd dived in with the knife that she'd had to battle to stop herself from drowning. Now she lay dead in the tube with the knife in her chest whilst Broocen struggled in the bloody fluid. The cord wrapped tighter and tighter around his neck.

Hurlen had quickly gone to the rescue after getting Odraine out, but was soon battling to save his own life as Broocen struggled to breathe and kept pulling him under and not allowing him to surface for air. Anjoy had joined Hurlen when she realized how scared Broocen was and was desperately trying to talk to him as Hurlen struggled to remove the cord, but the oxygen was slowly leaving Broocen's brain and he could barely hear her. As he breathed his last few breaths, he panicked and grabbed Anjoy. In the struggle she hit her head on the glass. The tube became bloodier as the blood poured from her wound.

Viola sobbed as she watched the tube getting redder and redder; now she couldn't see what was happening and only knew that two of her children were in there and she didn't know if they were dead or alive. She breathed a sigh of relief when Ashtez, Sirleen and Vonick joined her and prayed they could help. She smiled as Hurlen's head appeared, but then panicked as he screamed for help before disappearing again.

Ashtez climbed up the rope and pulled Hurlen up. In his arms he had Anjoy; blood was still pouring out of her head and her eyes were tightly closed. She struggled to hold onto them both and yelled down to Sirleen to help. Vonick passed the laser pin and searching wire to him and climbed up to them. He jumped in and took Anjoy out of Hurlen's arms, put her over his shoulder, then climbed down after Hurlen and Ashtez. He lay her on the floor and listened to her heart. He felt grief-stricken when he realized there was no sound. Sadly, he shook his head at Viola and Odraine.

Anjoy held Broocen's hand as they floated up. Whilst he smiled as the angels took them back to heaven and his beloved God, Anjoy wept. She so desperately wanted to stay with her parents.

Ashtez was on top of Anjoy, weeping at the loss of her beloved sister, who they'd desperately tried to save, and who would now never know what it was like to live with her family on the new planet. She was so looking forward to being with her. She spoke to God in her head as she wept.

"Why, God? Why have you taken Anjoy away from us? We were helping to free all your children and we wanted Anjoy to stay with us. Please, God, please send her back to us. We love her so much."

"It is Anjoy's choice. If she wishes to be with you then I will let her return," said God.

Ashtez barely heard God's reply as she sobbed into Anjoy's chest, or the people screaming as the Planet Force guards attacked them. She didn't notice the angels protecting them either, or Sirleen firing the laser pin at some of the guards whilst Vonick fired the searching wire at others. Guards lay on the floor all around them whilst Viola, Odraine, Hurlen and Ashtez all lay near Anjoy's body, weeping as they held her hands and stroked her face.

Anjoy smiled as she floated back down with the angels and entered her body. She yelled as she took her first deep breath of life and coughed up red fluid that she'd swallowed from the tube. Her family screamed with joy and all waited for Viola to finish hugging her so that they could do the same. Ashtez quickly thanked God for sending her beloved new sister back to them, not knowing that the rest of her family were doing the same. Vonick picked Anjoy up and carried her whilst Hurlen and Ashtez helped their parents to the porthole, desperate to get off the planet now.

God's angels were losing their battle against the dark angels and the sky was now so black that everyone struggled to see where they were going. Their breathing became more difficult as the air got thinner and thinner. Michael had now joined the fight and as he slew the dark angels the sky changed in places from black to red and the light would appear as God's other angels got through and lit it up for a short time before the dark angels took control once again.

Ashtez and Vonick used this light to guide their way to the porthole. Sirleen, having stopped to help one of the injured children, was now far behind. He almost dropped the child as one of the Planet Force guards stumbled into him in the darkness and, realizing it was the Spirit Master, hit him hard on the head.

Sirleen just in time remembered he still had the laser pin and fired it at the guard. As the guard fell down Sirleen struggled to continue walking and keep hold of the child. He was seeing double and he could barely focus because of the injury to his head, so he breathed a sigh of relief as his hand felt a different energy in the atmosphere. Relieved he'd found the porthole at last, he allowed himself and the child to fall into it.

Zut smiled as he watched. He'd been following Sirleen for quite a while now and couldn't believe his luck when he'd just disappeared with the child. Now he knew where the porthole was. He rushed to the same spot and fell into the hole, laughing with joy.

Chapter 35

PLANET TREHF
HOME

Rone stood in the same spot he'd left ten years ago and breathed the fresh air. It felt good to be home. He smiled as Governor Brent shook his hand and welcomed him home before he was taken to the City Care Unit to see what treatment he needed.

Cordelius was hugging Zeb and Samuel, and both had relieved smiles on their faces as they thanked God and his angels for sending him home safely. They'd been trying to astral travel and track him, but the dark energy had prevented them from entering the planet. Until they'd all arrived back, they had no idea if Cordelius was dead or alive.

Fiona was smiling as she watched her parents hugging and kissing and thanked God and the angels for bringing them back safely.

Anjoy stood with her parents and all the other angel children and stared at the strange but beautiful new planet that would not only be their new home, but also where they could finally live safely and openly talk to God.

God smiled as he looked down on his angel children, and Broocen smiled as he sat on God's lap with his warm and loving arms around him!

But was everyone safe and free?

Printed in the United Kingdom
by Lightning Source UK Ltd.
104317UKS00001B/356